Kidnapped and
lion, Leowulf, l
Norman lady A
tamely to such
captor at every
freedom, and
Normandy at the side of her ~~~
Brec.

But to Leowulf, Adela is the means to make his peace with William of Normandy, King and conqueror of his country. He will do anything to force Adela to stay with him—even if it means making her his wife....

...held as a hostage by the Saxon
...ord of Eriuwald ... The proud
...dela de Lisc refuses to submit
...rough treatment. Defying her
...turn, she fights furiously for her
...her right to return in peace to
...her ... her beloved Guy de

Lady in the Lion's Den

Elaine Reeve

MILLS & BOON LIMITED
London · Sydney · Toronto

First published in Great Britain 1980
by Mills & Boon Limited, 15–16 Brook's Mews,
London W1Y 1LF

© Elaine Reeve 1980

Australian copyright 1980
Philippine copyright 1980

ISBN 0 263 73234 7

The text of this publication or any part thereof may not be
reproduced or transmitted in any form or by any means,
electronic or mechanical, including photocopying,
recording, storage in an information retrieval system, or
otherwise, without the written permission of the publisher.

This book is sold subject to the condition that it shall not,
by way of trade or otherwise, be lent, resold, hired out or
otherwise circulated without the prior consent of the publisher in any form of binding or cover other than that in
which it is published and without a similar condition
including this condition being imposed on the subsequent
purchaser.

Set in VIP Times 12 on 12½pt
by Fakenham Press Limited

Printed and bound in Great Britain by
Cox & Wyman Ltd, Reading

CHAPTER
ONE

ADELA'S bedchamber was in total darkness, and she forced her limbs to relax beneath the furs that covered her. The alien sound that had awoken her seemed to have ceased—if, indeed, it had existed at all, for she had slept lightly these past six weeks, and thought sometimes that the sound of her own breathing was enough to wake her.

The reason for her unease was that her uncle, Sir Edward de Lise, had been called away to help quell the unrest further south, and left Erinwald with only a minimum of men to protect it. Nothing had happened to justify her nervousness, however, and now that the King was back in England after his eight-month absence in Normandy, surely her uncle would soon return.

It had been a trying time for her. The sound of her uncle's young wife, Marguerite, admonishing one or other of the Saxons in a petulant, peevish voice had grown more frequent as the weeks went by and Adela, who spoke the Saxon tongue fluently, usually had to intervene to sort out misunderstandings and soothe ruffled tempers. Marguerite made little attempt to master the language herself, and the Saxons who understood a few words of French refused to admit the fact to her. Adela held her peace about it. She was hopelessly in the middle, owing some loyalty to Marguerite and yet sympathising whole-heartedly with the Saxons.

A rift had developed between the two girls—at twenty-three, Marguerite was but four years Adela's senior—caused mainly because Adela's command of the Saxon tongue gave her an advantage which the other considered undermined her position as mistress of the manor. Adela did her best to keep things cordial between them, for she had known 'Margo' long before her uncle had wed her, and counted her a friend; but it was becoming more and more difficult.

She had never wanted to come to England anyway. When the Duke had taken his army across the Channel to wrest the crown from Earl Harold, her father and her uncle had gone with him, leaving her with her ageing grand-mother.

When her father had been killed at Hastings, cloven in two by a Saxon axe, nothing would have induced Adela to leave her beloved Normandy to cross the Channel to join her uncle in that barbaric land. Later, with William crowned, Marguerite had gone to join her husband and Adela had been content to remain with her grandmother. That elderly lady's sudden death only weeks later, however, had changed the course of her life.

Had things been different, and she less reluctant to marry the man of her father's choice, no doubt she would have been wed and settled long since. As it was, she had no other family and knew she could not accept a home with friends without feeling herself a burden upon them. So she had sent word to her uncle, seen her grandmother buried, and when she could put it off no longer, made the journey to England in the dreadful weather of mid-February.

There she had found her uncle and Marguerite firmly installed at Erinwald, the manor and lands given to Sir Edward by William soon after his coronation at Christmas. Although she had now been at Erinwald for ten months, and was resigned to England, Adela still cherished the hope that one day she would return to Normandy.

In those first unhappy weeks Guy de Brec, a chevalier in her uncle's entourage, had been a sympathetic friend, and a fondness had quickly developed between them. He talked often of returning to Normandy, and more than once the thought had passed through Adela's mind that they might come to marry and go back together. Guy was with Sir Edward, and she had missed him these past six weeks.

She turned over on to her side, hunching the furs around her against the December cold, and allowed thoughts of Guy to lull her back to the edges of sleep.

A door slamming open further down the gallery brought her upright in the bed, catching her breath at the sound of footsteps outside. Wide-eyed and with a thudding heart, she stared towards her own door, and suddenly, with a resounding crash that brought a cry of fear to her lips, it was flung wide. The man—a Saxon—stood framed in the glow from the torch thrust into the wall-sconce outside.

'Dress yourself,' he commanded.

Fear drove the power of movement away, although she understood him well enough.

He advanced into the room, grasped her arm and before she had time to protest, dragged her from the bed and left her in a heap on the floor. He picked up the clothes she had discarded earlier and thrust them towards her. There was no mistaking his meaning when he repeated his command.

Agitated cries from the chamber next door told her that Marguerite was suffering similarly. Her head buzzed with questions, but she dared not disobey. The Saxon withdrew a few feet and stood waiting, obviously meaning to watch her dress; she stood up, turned away from his gaze and pulled the gown over the gossamer-thin garment in which she had slept. Shivering with cold, she struggled with the loops and her trembling fingers fumbled as she fastened the gold filigree girdle about her slender waist.

Her eyes swept the room frantically even as she finished dressing, but her jewel-handled knife was on the carved oak table on the other side of the bed and she could not hope to reach it. A Saxon girl, Frida, came in just then. She had a twisted leg and moved awkwardly, and she came in for the worst of Marguerite's ill-humour; so Adela had made an effort to befriend her. Now she came in with an apologetic glance and began to collect together some of Adela's clothes.

The Saxon snatched up the heavy mantle and held it out to her. 'Come,' he growled and caught her arm, half-dragging her out to the gallery.

She found her voice at last as she struggled to get free. 'Let me go, you oaf! What are you doing? Where are you taking me? How dare you——!' But he was far stronger, and fighting him only sapped the energy she might need later. She was too afraid to think of the Saxon words and he ignored her protests, pulling her heedlessly towards the stairs.

As she went down, the scene that met Adela's eyes made her heart sink and she clenched her fists in helpless fury. The men she and Marguerite had left drinking and talking so jovially when they retired to their chambers, were all slumped where they sat, drugged and unconscious, being bound hand and foot by a few of the Saxons. Ailsa, Marguerite's hand-maiden, was on her knees in the rushes with her hands bound in front of her.

Anger burned in Adela at the treachery of the Saxons within the manor, who had obviously had a hand in this and opened wide the doors. How could they do it? They had been fairly treated by Sir Edward all these months....

She had her answer almost immediately as her eyes were drawn to a figure standing with his back to the fire, his legs apart, his arms folded across his chest, surveying the scene with grim satisfaction. She did not doubt that it was Leowulf. Leowulf, who had been lord of Erinwald before the Norman invasion.

All the lands of those who had fought for Harold had, of course, been forfeit to William, but after his coronation he had allowed lands to be restored to the Saxon owners who had survived, for a payment of gold and silver. But it had never been paid for Erinwald. Adela had learned that it was because all the wealth of Erinwald had been given to Harold to help pay the costs of raising the sort of army needed to keep out William's hordes.

Tall, broad and powerful, perhaps thirty years old, Leowulf stood in the torchlight of the great hall and his shaggy hair and beard were a fiery gold; she could understand why they called him 'the lion'. There was something about him that would brook no opposition, and she found her anger directed at him instead of those serfs who dared not defy him.

Anger, however, could not prevent an icy tremor of fear sliding over her as her captor pulled her roughly towards this man, wrenched her arm violently and sent her tumbling, with a cry of indignation and pain, to the rushes at his feet.

Leowulf laughed softly. 'Nay, Olwyn, not so rough. We don't want to bruise the wench. Damaged merchandise is no use to us.'

Adela's face gave no sign that she had understood these words, but inwardly she shivered a little at the contempt in his voice and the veiled threat behind his words. His foot nudged her, and when she looked up into glinting blue eyes, he gestured her to stand.

As she did so, Marguerite was brought struggling down the stairs. When she saw Leowulf, she too guessed his identity and let forth a stream of angry protests and demands for instant release.

'Woman, be silent!' the Saxon thundered, and Marguerite was so surprised to hear his French command that she did, indeed, cease her furious tirade. 'Bind them quickly,' he said in his own language to the man Olwyn. 'We've tarried long enough.' He turned and strode out with a command flung over his shoulder for the others to follow him.

When he had gone, the man who held Marguerite tried to steal a kiss and the struggle that ensued drew Olwyn's attention. With a muttered curse, he strode swiftly towards them and pulled the man away. 'Are you a fool, Edgar? Leowulf will have you skinned—bind her and curb your lusts!'

With his attention momentarily diverted, Adela seized her chance and ran; but the Saxon was faster and in an instant brought her crashing down, her face in the rushes. With an oath, he held her down with his knee in her back and wrenched her arms above her head. He bound her wrists tightly with a rough rope and then hauled her to her feet. Winded and shaken, she stood trembling before him and was helpless as he pulled her roughly towards the door.

Outside there must have been nearly two-score horses, and mounted on many of them were Saxons Adela recognised, one or two of the women with babes and young children. Clearly Leowulf did not intend to leave anyone at Erinwald to face the wrath of Sir Edward de Lise.

Olwyn took both her and Marguerite to Leowulf. 'Do they ride, lord?'

Leowulf glanced at Adela's stormy face and bound wrists, and then at Marguerite, who was trying in vain to break free of Olwyn's iron grip. He shook his head. 'Nay. Take the lady Marguerite up with you. I doubt anyone else could hold her and she must not be harmed. I'll take this wench. Come, 'tis more than time we were gone.'

He lifted Adela on to his grey horse as if she weighed no more than a feather and mounted behind her, and as it seemed futile to resist, she withdrew into a dignified silence. Far better she conserve her energy for some more likely opportunity of escape. Marguerite's protests and cries for release met with little response from Olwyn, and it was Leowulf, as he led the procession away fron Erinwald, who eventually cut across her shrill voice with a curt, 'Cease your prattle, woman, lest you wish your mouth bound as well as your hands!'

Much to Adela's relief, Marguerite subsided into angry silence, and much to her surprise, Leowulf wrapped a bearskin around her against the cold. But she could draw no comfort from such solicitude. What she knew of him by hearsay was enough to leave her cold with apprehension.

He was a man with a reputation amongst the Saxons as a great warrior, supposedly a friend of Earl Harold's, and one who had fought like a hellion at Hastings. He had surrendered his people at Erinwald to Sir Edward de Lise and then fled to the hills with about a third of his men, and the hills had been his sanctuary ever since.

From there he swooped down upon small bands of Normans who strayed too close, although he stopped short of inflicting physical harm on de Lise men—no doubt fearing reprisals on the Saxons he left at Erinwald

—Adela herself had witnessed the return of one luckless group. The Saxon had had them tied to the saddle facing their horses' tails and sent them back with flowers in their hair and garlands round their necks; and the deaths of several Normans from other villages and manors in the area were attributed to Leowulf's hand.

It was not a comforting thought.

The procession rode for some miles at a steady pace. The rope was so tight around Adela's wrists that it bit savagely into her flesh, but she made no complaint for she doubted it would avail her anything. After some time she did pluck up enough courage to venture a question: 'What will happen to our men at Erinwald, Saxon?' she asked. 'Sir Edward——'

'You have knowledge of our language, wench,' he interrupted curtly. 'Use it.'

Her eyes flew to his face, but his gaze was on the way ahead and he did not look at her. She toyed for a moment with the idea of denying her knowledge and pretending she had not understood him, but immediately knew it would be folly. Obviously he had been kept well informed. So she repeated her question rather resentfully, and added: 'Sir Edward may not return for days—weeks....'

'Do you take me for a fool, wench?' he demanded, glancing at her with raised eyebrows. 'I made sure Sir Edward was but a day's

ride away before I moved. I've no wish to be
burdened with you longer than I must.'

She digested this silently for a moment, and
then asked, 'We are hostages, then? And you
intend to release us as soon as possible?'

'Peace, wench,' he said wearily. 'You will
know soon enough. We have a long ride and I
must keep my attention on it. Save your questions.'

They kept up the pace, heading, of course,
into the hills. Although Adela strained her eyes
into the heavy darkness seeking some land-
mark that would identify their route, the night
was moonless and she could see only shapeless
shadows, and soon gave up. Strange creatures
scuttled away before the advancing horses; in
the darkness a wolf howled and Adela shivered
at the inhuman sound. There were a few words
spoken between the Saxons, and only the
thrumming of horses' hooves disturbed the
eerie silence of the night.

Her cloak and the bearskin kept her warm,
but sitting sideways, with her hands tied before
her and only the Saxon's strong arms preventing her from slipping off, she was far from
comfortable. She had begun by endeavouring
to keep her seat without his support, for she
cringed away from contact with him; but it put
such a strain on her that she yielded a little to
lean against his arm and chest.

The pain in her wrists grew worse and her
hands tingled with numbness; yet she bore all

her discomforts with fortitude and in silence, praying all the while for a miracle in the way of rescue. Or, failing rescue, that at least the end of the journey was near.

She lost all notion of time and distance, but the eastern sky was lightening when her captor reined his horse to a standstill.

The place to which they had been brought was a long, low building, dimly lit from within, and Adela could see the outlines of several smaller buildings close by.

The door swung open and two men emerged, calling greetings. Leowulf sprang easily from the saddle and lifted her down, giving one or two casual orders concerning the comfort of those Saxons he had brought from Erinwald, before gesturing Olwyn to bring Marguerite.

Inside, Adela glanced briefly round the hall. It was a rough wooden building, with ill-worked hangings on the walls taking off a little of the starkness, and she guessed it had been hastily built when they fled from Erinwald. The floor was strewn with pallets, for the most part unslept on, but a few men raised themselves on their elbows to view their lord and pass comments on the success of his mission. A table laden with food and drinking horns stood against the wall, and at the far end were two curtained doorways, presumably leading through to kitchens and bedchambers.

She shot a nervous look at Marguerite and encountered in her eyes the same fearful ten-

sion she felt within herself. They were entirely
at the mercy of their captors and could only
pray that Leowulf would consider it politic to
ensure they came to no harm. She would
dearly have liked to give way to tears pricking
her eyes at the pain in her wrists, but condemned herself for such weakness and strove
to pull herself together, for she might yet
need all her wits and strength to fight off the
lusty Saxon heathens.

But it seemed it would not come to that. She
and Marguerite were taken through one curtained doorway and put into separate chambers, with a warning that to try to escape would
be futile, as they would be guarded well.
Leowulf lifted the torch from the wall-sconce in
the room given to Adela, remarked drily that
he would not have her set the place afire, and
made to withdraw.

She started forward, with a catch of desperation in her voice. 'Please——' She had hoped
he might at least free her hands once there was
no chance of escape, for she did not know how
much longer she could bear the burning pain
caused by the rope Olwyn had tied so cruelly
tight. But she stopped abruptly. Would she
weep at a little discomfort and ask him to loose
her bonds like any weakling maid?

She fought the tears and squared her
shoulders, lifting her chin. No, she was Adela
de Lise, and she would show these Saxon barbarians that the ladies of Normandy were made

of sterner stuff. ''Tis nothing,' she said, and turned haughtily away.

'What?' he mocked. 'Are you afraid of the dark, Proud One?'

She bit back the angry retort that came to her lips and said coldly, 'If you would do me a kindness, Saxon, pray relieve me of your presence!'

With an impatient sound, he put up the torch and strode across to her, pulling her arm to turn her towards him.

She could not help the cry that escaped her as the pain shot through the raw place on her wrists. She bit her lips together, and kept her eyes downcast lest the tears should spill, but he raised her chin and his hard blue eyes searched her face. Then he looked down at her hands. With an oath, he drew her to the light and raised her arms, and what he saw brought a scowl to his face. He cursed Olwyn with words she did not understand, but with a force that sent a tremor through her.

'He did but serve you, Saxon,' she said as she raised her head, and added scornfully, 'Had he bound me any looser, I should not now be here!'

At that, he threw back his head and laughed. 'Bravely said, wench! But it does not serve me to have you bearing tales of ill-usage back with you.'

It was on the tip of her tongue to demand what he termed being dragged from their beds in the middle of the night, tied up and carried off into the hills, if not ill-usage; but she wisely refrained and instead raised her brown eyes to his and asked coolly: 'So you will let us go?'

He drew out his knife, toying with it thoughtfully for a moment before raising it slowly to her throat. He looked at her, his eyes glittering, and said caressively, 'That would depend whether or not I get what I want, pretty one.'

She did not shrink from him but smiled and shook her head. 'Nay, Saxon,' she said with a calm she was far from feeling. 'Save your threats. I will guess it's Erinwald you want, and your words a moment ago made it plain you will not touch us till at least you have an answer. And if it is not Erinwald, whatever the reason for this—this outrage, and whatever the outcome, my uncle will hunt you down and it will go ill with you if we have met with less than respect at your hands.'

Leowulf chuckled. ''Tis a clever tongue you have, wench, and a brave one,' he mocked. 'But do not credit me with virtues I may not have.' He lowered the knife and cut the rope that bound her wrists.

With a little gasp, she flexed her fingers gingerly, wincing as the blood flowed back into her hands and little darts of pain shot through the raw places. 'My thanks, Saxon,' she murmured drily. 'Your man does not know his strength, I think.'

'He knows it well enough,' Leowulf sheathed his knife and turned towards the door. 'I will send someone with a salve.'

He went out, taking the torch but leaving the door open to admit the light from outside. Suddenly feeling tired and drained, Adela sat down on the bed, and in a few minutes Frida came in bearing a wooden box. She thrust her thoughts and fears away to be dealt with later and submitted silently as the girl gently applied the cool, soothing salve. Frida kept her eyes averted, casting fleeting almost nervous glances at her, but Adela felt disinclined to say anything kind to her and was glad when she was finished.

Alone in the darkness, she lay down on the bed, pulled the pelts over her and closed her eyes. Prisoners of Leowulf! The effrontery of the man! He had not denied it was Erinwald he wanted, and it seemed fairly obvious he intended to exchange them for the manor, but surely he was not fool enough to believe it would work? What did he hope to gain? During the King's absence in Normandy unrest had flared in England, which although it had been quelled for the most part, would surely not encourage William to deal lightly with upstarts like Leowulf. And to demand Erinwald back, having abducted de Lise's wife and niece ... Was the man a fool?

She turned over on her side, and clenched her fist. Whatever the Saxon wanted, it put her uncle in an impossible position. And Guy....

Thoughts of Guy were like a balm to her troubled mind; fears and speculation, anger and indignation all faded under the image of his dark, handsome face.

Eventually she slept, but only to dream that her uncle and Guy and a score of men rode up on white horses, slew the Saxons, put torches to the buildings and carried her and Marguerite to safety in the haven of their arms. She looked back over Guy's shoulder and glimpsed for an instant the bearded face of Leowulf at one of the windows, before the flames leapt up and consumed him.

CHAPTER
TWO

LITTLE light penetrated the room through the thick skin at the small window, but the sound of activity both outside and within the building indicated that it was now broad daylight. Sleep had fled from Adela when she woke abruptly from her dream, and she pushed the pelts away and sat up.

She started as the door opened suddenly, but it was only Frida, who brought water for her to wash with and an armful of clothes. 'I have brought you some of your clothes, my lady,' she said. 'Let me help you dress. Are your wrists soothed?'

'Yes, thank you, Frida. The soreness is greatly relieved.' She shed her kirtle and washed quickly, grateful for the coldness of the water that drove away the last remnants of sleep and the lingering, ragged edges of her dream. 'Do you know what Leowulf intends with us?'

'No, my lady.'

And I doubt, she thought, that you would tell me even if you did know. 'Well then, am I to be allowed to see the Lady Marguerite?'

Frida helped her put on her soft gown of a

gold colour and said unhappily, 'I don't know. Perhaps if you ask my lord...'

' "My lord"?' Adela echoed in disgust. 'Why, only yesterday you referred to Sir Edward as "my lord" and owned him such. Your loyalties are very thin!'

Frida shook her head and said, almost defiantly, 'I am Saxon, lady. My lord is Leowulf and has always been. We owned Sir Edward lord for a time because Leowulf wished it.'

Adela could not prevent the sound of contempt that escaped her and she turned away with a cautionary, 'That is dangerous talk, Frida.' But Frida, unperturbed, began to comb her long dark hair, and said nothing.

Adela had no chance to say anything more, for the door burst open and Leowulf strode in. It was all she could do to restrain herself from letting forth a gurgle of derisive laughter at the sight of him, because one side of his face was marred from cheekbone to beard with three deep, bloody scratches and it was obvious that some female had got the better of him.

The glance of icy fire he sent her sobered her instantly and she withdrew hastily across the room as he commanded Frida to 'Put something on these accurs'd scratches!' She watched while he submitted impatiently to the girl's nervous application of the salve that had been used on her own wrists, and was startled when he suddenly looked directly at her from

beneath scowling brows and said forcefully:
'Your uncle's wife is a fool!'

For a moment, wide-eyed in astonishment,
Adela could do no more than stare at him.
Then: 'Margo did that?' A flicker of apprehension. 'What did you do to her?'

'Do?' he roared. 'Do? I? I meant only to cut
her bonds. But when my knife was through, she
was at me like a demented wildcat. I tell you,
'tis a wonder she lives still—had she been a
man, I would——'

'Of that I have no doubt, Saxon,' she interrupted boldly, 'for I have heard of your skills
with the axe! And,' she hurried on, aware of the
scowling expression on his face, and yet unable
to prevent herself goading him further, 'I
should not have thought a mere scratch or two
would cause such a strong and fearless man as
yourself so much concern. Does a lion trouble
himself over a mere wildcat?'

She thought, for one terrible moment, that
she had gone too far; with an abrupt movement
of his head towards the door, he dismissed
Frida, and Adela, suddenly afraid to be alone
with him, tried to detain her with a request for
some of the salve for her wrists. Leowulf, however, cut her short with an impatient, 'Later,'
and Frida limped out.

He sat down in the straight-backed chair,
and looking towards her, gestured the floor at
his feet. 'Come. Sit here.' Then, as she hesitated, added in some annoyance: 'I'll not bite

you, wench!'

Reluctantly, feeling a little like a hound called to sit at his master's feet and wondering if that was his intention, she did as he bade her with as much dignity as she could muster.

He leaned back, lifted one leg to rest his leather-clad foot on the edge of the chair, and with one arm lying carelessly across his uplifted knee, he regarded her through half-closed eyes. It crossed her mind that a lion might watch his prey in just that deceptively lazy manner. He was well dubbed 'the lion'.

'How is it you speak our tongue so fluently?' he asked and although there was no hostility in his voice, he had an unfortunate way of speaking—or perhaps it was just the way he looked—that seemed always to veil a threat of dire consequences if one should fail to answer.

She did not want to tell him anything, but thought that perhaps if she could lure him into talking, he might reveal something of his plans. She might learn something which later could be used to bring him to justice and the end he deserved.

'My grandmother,' she said. 'It was well known in Normandy—ever since the Confessor promised England's crown to William if he should die without issue—that our Duke would be King of this realm. And she—my grandmother—being herself half Saxon, set about teaching me the language, for she said it might be a great asset to me. When the Duke later left to take England from Harold's usurping hold,' she went on, well aware that such words were likely to anger a man who had been so staunchly for Harold and his claim to the throne, 'I was left with her, and we spoke only Saxon to each other.'

He made no comment and was silent for a long moment. Then: 'Have you met with William?'

The question, and the suddenness with which he asked it, surprised her. 'The King? Yes, but twice only, and we exchanged no more than a few words of courtesy.'

Silent and thoughtful, he seemed to stare unseeingly beyond her. 'Think you he would accept my hand between his?'

Startled, and feeling a strange inclination to laugh at him, she met the piercing gaze he turned on her and realised that he was serious. 'You want to pledge yourself to William? After all you have done against him?'

He made a slight dismissive gesture. 'I weary of it. These hillside skirmishes gain us nothing. I have not been alone in hoping someone would emerge from amongst us to oppose William and restore England to Saxon, but——'

'Not yourself, my lord?' she taunted. 'Did you not fancy the crown on your own head? You have quite a reputation amongst your own kind, I think. You fought beside Harold and were owned his friend—you have, they say, the strength and pride and courage of the lion they call you.'

'Nay, nay,' he laughed. 'Not for me the politics of kingship; I have no taste for its subtleties and intrigues—nor so devious a mind! And now,' he shrugged, ''tis too late. William's hold is too firm on this land of ours and he seems a man well fitted to rule. I will better serve my fellow Saxons now by ceasing these useless games and pledging my arm for William and a united England. Others would follow my lead.'

He paused and went on, 'But my price is that I should be allowed to return unhindered and unmolested as lord of Erinwald. . . . What think you? Would William hold my life forfeit if I went to him thus?'

Adela shook her head. 'How should I know that? But...' She looked away for a moment and then raised her eyes. 'I have heard it said that if a man comes to him who has worked against him in the past, William will forgive all his crimes and wrongs if he believes he can trust his loyalty for the future. But 'tis also said that he is seldom wrong in his judgement of a man, so you must not go to him if treachery is in your heart, for you'll not deceive him.'

For a moment, Leowulf was silent, but his eyes narrowed slightly and it was impossible to guess his thoughts. Then, unsmiling but with a twinkle of amusement in his eyes: 'Nay, but I go to William in good faith, though I thank you for the warning!'

She flushed at the mockery in his voice, and felt a rising anger overcome her caution. 'What need was there to take us?' she demanded. 'You seem to have everything planned—your allegiance in return for Erinwald. Why do you need us?'

'Because,' he said in the tone of one explaining something extremely simple to a backward child, 'William has just returned to find that England is not as peaceful as he would wish it. And I am not so sure of his good will that I'll walk into the wolf's lair without first ensuring that the wolf is not hungry for Saxon blood. Your presence assures me of words with your uncle who, I am told, is close enough to the King to be sure of a hearing. If William admits that a living Saxon prepared to aid him is more use to him than a dead one, he and I shall deal well together.'

'You think he will deal at all with a man who fled to the hills and abandoned his people to the mercy of their conquerors?' she demanded contemptuously.

'What?' he retorted. 'Would you have had me see my people slain? If we had made a stand and fought de Lise when he came to take Erinwald, how many of my Saxons would have been killed? How much damage done to the property? Do you think we would have won? Even had we driven them away, others would have come.'

He paused for a moment, and then went on, 'William himself uses craft more often than he uses force, and I doubt not he will see the thinking behind mine. I was sure de Lise could control his men and was not intent only on rape, plunder and killing like most of his kind. He knew that if he allowed me to leave, I would take with me all those who could not stomach a Norman lord—those who would doubtless cause him trouble. To fight led only to defeat. This way, there is victory of a kind. And,' he added and more to himself than to her, 'I have something in mind to add weight to my side of the bargain.'

Adela raised her head and her brown eyes challenged him. 'You are very sure you will have your way, Saxon.'

He raised an eyebrow and regarded her with a flicker of a smile lifting a corner of his mouth and a gleam of speculation in his eyes. 'Yea, little one,' he said softly, letting his gaze roam insolently over her. 'And more so now than before, I think.'

She flushed darkly, flinching from the mockery in his eyes. 'I would like,' she said quickly, saying the first thing that came into her mind, 'to see Marguerite.'

He stood up immediately. 'Come.' Without pausing to see if she followed him, he strode to the door, threw it open and disappeared outside, leaving her to scramble to her feet and run

after him, thrusting away the horrible feeling of
having been somehow degraded by his roaming
gaze.

He was standing at the door of Marguerite's
chamber, holding it open for her, and when she
moved past him into the room he stood watching her.

'Margo!' Marguerite was lying on the bed,
tied hand and foot and with an expression on
her face that anyone who knew her as Adela
did, would instantly recognise as a portent of
the fury raging within.

Adela spun round and glared at the Saxon.
'You cannot keep her tied up like this!' she
cried, and was so infuriated by the amusement
in his eyes that she added coldly, 'Are you so
afraid of a woman that you must keep her
bound helpless so that she cannot hurt you?
Your courage has been greatly exaggerated, I
think!'

'Nay, wench,' he said calmly, ''tis not my
courage you should doubt, but my temper. I've
no wish to harm the lady, but unless she keeps
her claws well hidden I cannot guarantee her
safety. Perhaps you can persuade her to curb
her wildcat instincts.' He inclined his head with
a mocking smile and withdrew, leaving them
alone.

Adela turned back and dropped to her knees
beside the bed. 'Oh, Margo, you should not
have scratched him. There is nothing to be
done yet.'

'You, no doubt, have been so honey-sweet to these—these barbarians,' Marguerite snapped, 'that your comfort is assured!' Her malevolent gaze swept over the younger girl accusingly, taking in her free hands, the fresh gown and newly-combed hair.

'Oh!' Hurt and indignant, Adela sat back on her heels and looked at her aunt. 'How can you say such a thing? He untied me when we got here because that brute, Olwyn, tied me so tight he nearly severed my wrists!' To prove it, she held out her arms to display the red marks. 'He will release you too if you will calm down a little. We'll gain nothing by making things worse for ourselves. If we must be prisoners here, we may as well be comfortable.'

She sat on the edge of the bed and tried to undo the knots that bound her aunt. 'Uncle Edward is but a day's ride away,' she said, 'and I have also discovered what it is the Saxon wants.' In as few words as possible, she told her of the conversation with Leowulf, realising as she did so that she had really found out nothing that he had not wanted her to know.

Marguerite's reaction was a contemptuous, 'Hah! He digs his own grave then, for William will never agree! He is not a fool.'

Adela was conscious of a pang of apprehension. She did not think Leowulf had seriously considered the possibility of being refused, and if he were to be refused . . . She gave up struggling with the knots and looked at Marguerite. 'I think we had better hope the King does agree, Margo. I fear for our very lives if the Saxon is denied.'

'He dares not do anything beyond threatening us,' Marguerite said, although without any real conviction in her voice. 'That would do very little to further his cause! And Edward will not allow anything to happen to us.'

The morning passed slowly. Adela could make no impression on the knots, and Marguerite finally declared that even if she had to apologise to Leowulf for scratching him, she would make him release her.

Towards midday, Frida came in bearing food and water. She set it down and then stood, hesitant, looking at Adela. Abruptly, she drew a small, slender knife from the folds of her gown and held it out.

'Take this,' she said quickly. 'There are two horses, tethered in the trees. My lord has gone hunting, but to the north—you must ride south. You will soon recognise the way. I can do no more.'

A moment later she was gone, leaving Adela staring in amazement at the knife in her hands.

'What is it?' Marguerite demanded.

Adela turned and held up the knife with an almost triumphant smile, and as she moved to cut the ropes that bound her, translated Frida's words. 'We must hurry,' she added, and leaving Marguerite rubbing her wrists, went to the door and peeped out. At the end of the gallery one of the Saxon men she did not know stood with his arms folded, his long-bladed knife thrust into his belt.

She closed the door, and looked across at the window. 'We'll have to go out that way.' Unlike Erinwald, there were no shutters at the windows here, only thick skins fastened across the inside. While Marguerite wrapped up the food Frida had brought, Adela pulled over the only chair in the room, climbed up on it and began to cut at the skin.

It took but a few minutes, and although the opening was not large, both girls were slightly built and slid through fairly easily, to tumble inelegantly to the ground outside and run for the cover of the trees.

They found the horses a little distance away, each with a wolf pelt across the saddle, and Adela, clutching the little knife, silently blessed Frida and prayed Leowulf did not discover who had helped them. Wrapped up against the cold, and being as quiet as possible, they led the horses through the trees to the rough track beyond, mounted and rode quickly away.

They rode hard for about half an hour before slowing to a trot and exchanging smiles of relief and satisfaction. Adela let out a gurgle of laughter. 'Now that arrogant Saxon must find another way to make his peace with the King!'

It was Marguerite who, for some reason, half-turned her head and glanced back the way they had come. 'Oh, no! Adela . . .'

There were a handful of horsemen, close enough to be identifiable as Saxons, and they were closing the gap relentlessly. 'We cannot outride them!' Marguerite cried.

Something tightened inside Adela. 'Try!' she shouted, and dug her heels into the horse's flanks. The ground slid away beneath them alarmingly, and all Adela knew was the drumming of horses' hooves and the pounding of blood in her ears.

But it was useless, of course. Leowulf and his men were soon all around them, blocking their way and flanking them on either side. Drawing their horses to an abrupt standstill, the two girls faced Leowulf and Olwyn, and Adela was conscious of the racing of her heart as she looked at Leowulf; his face was expressionless, but his eyes were flint-hard, glinting with anger.

Shifting her gaze to Olwyn, she was startled to find him regarding her with something she might almost have thought was amusement. Strangely, it was he and not his lord, who spoke. Inclining his head to indicate the way they had come, he said drily: 'Back, my lady, if you please.'

She shot him a venomous look, and was about to tell him just what she thought of that, when Marguerite, who could guess what Olwyn had said, murmured, 'Adela, we cannot fight them all, and to try would, I fear, be very unwise.'

The look Adela gave her aunt was even more

expressive than the one she had sent Olwyn, but, wrenching the horse's rein viciously, she turned him round and with her eyes fixed steadily on the way ahead and her head held high, she said not one word as the procession made its way back to the Saxons' hideaway.

CHAPTER
THREE

IT was drawing towards dusk when they arrived
back at the wooden building which Adela was
beginning to think of as 'the den', and inside
the torches were being lit from the blazing fire
and put into sconces, sending shadows across
the hall.

Her heart sank to see Frida seated alone at
the long table, for it could only mean that
Leowulf knew it was she who had helped them.
She did not even glance up as Olwyn escorted
them towards the curtained doorway, but when
Leowulf came in, she raised her eyes and
watched him walk to the fire with such a look of
fear in her eyes that Adela felt her own
apprehension grow. The Saxon stood with his
back to the fire and said grimly, 'Frida. Come
here.'

Adela turned abruptly and pulled her arm
from Olwyn's grip. 'What is he going to do?'
she whispered as the young girl, with trepidation clearly etched on her elfin face, rose and
limped across the hall. Beneath the cover of the
wolf-pelt she still clutched around her, Adela
pressed the little knife into Marguerite's hand.

Olwyn shook his head. 'I do not know. But

he is not in a good humour. Come.'

'Nay!' She evaded his arm, and started forward. 'Leowulf!' She walked boldly up to him, determined he was not going to get away with punishing Frida. 'Frida is not to blame for our escape,' she said, deliberately speaking French. 'And you cannot punish her for it.'

The Saxon raised an eyebrow, his expression unreadable. A hush seemed to have fallen in the hall, even though only one or two had understood what she said. They knew Leowulf and not one of them would dare confront him when he was in such a humour, nor speak to him in such a tone. But there were also those who knew the Lady Adela, and were not so surprised that *she* had dared.

Leowulf's eyes glinted. 'Can I not? You presume too much, I think. She aided your escape and thus betrayed me——'

'But she helped us merely because——'

'I know,' he interrupted curtly, 'why she did it. There is little that went on at Erinwald that I do not know. It excuses nothing.'

'You cannot punish her!' she persisted. 'She—she found her loyalties divided, that is all.' Guilt lent a pleading note to her voice. 'I think it is my fault, for I made her feel badly that she—and the others who have been at Erinwald these past months—betrayed our trust in them in such a way. You, after all, have done little for them in that time. If anyone should be punished, 'tis I.'

She paused, her head came up and her brown eyes met his steadily. 'I allowed her to take the risk of helping us, knowing how it would be for her when you discovered it. Please, I beg you, do not hurt her.'

A look, almost of satisfaction, came into his face. He reached out and pulled her towards him, pushing away the wolf pelt as it slipped, and bruising the flesh of her shoulders with his fingers.

She drew a sharp breath, and ignoring her futile struggles, his mouth came down on hers in a cruel, demanding, passionless kiss that drove the breath from her body and left her shaking.

He released her abruptly, and regarded her with the merest trace of sardonic amusement lifting a corner of his mouth as she glared her anger and resentment at him and raised her hand to touch her sore lips.

He turned to Frida and told her to take herself to the kitchen and stay there until he sent for her. The he glanced across at Olwyn. 'Take them and tie them up. I'll have no more trouble from either of them!'

Adela, silently fuming, turned and walked back to Olwyn and Marguerite, flushed and angry, feeling humiliated, yet holding her head high and refusing to look at any of the Saxons standing about in the hall.

As Olwyn led them into the passageway beyond the curtain, Adela felt the hilt of the

knife pressed back into her hand. Obviously
Marguerite did not want to be found with it!
Silently cursing her for her cowardice, she held
it carefully out of sight in the folds of her gown
as Olwyn tied Marguerite's hands, loosely but
securely, and left her in the room from which
they had earlier escaped. Wryly she noted that
the skin at the window had been replaced by a
shutter, fastened from the outside.

Olwyn propelled her along to the bedchamber next door, his hand gripping her
shoulder, firm yet not unduly hard.

Inside, she sat down on the bed, careful to sit
on the knife, and noted that here, too, there
was now a shutter at the window. Olwyn took
her hands to tie them up, but when he saw the
marks on her wrists he paused and raised his
eyes to hers. For an absurd moment she
thought he was going to apologise for hurting
her the last time; but instead he bent down and
proceeded to tie his rope around one ankle.
Then, leaving enough to enable her to move
her feet, tied it round the other. He fastened
the end of the rope to the bed, and departed
with a wry grin at the look of fury on her face.

When he had gone, she twisted round and
retrieved the knife, but as she turned it over in
her hands, the sound of voices outside made
her thrust it quickly beneath the pelts on the
bed and turn back innocently just as Leowulf
entered.

He raised an eyebrow at the rope around

her ankle, and glancing at her wrists, made some disgruntled comment about Olwyn being far too soft. 'Frida gave you a knife,' he said. 'Do you have it still?'

She looked up into his unsmiling face and for an agonising moment her mind went blank. Then she pulled herself together and slowly shook her head. 'No. I ... I don't know what happened to it.'

His expression was grim, and he turned to the door. 'Then perhaps I can persuade Frida to recall what she did with it.'

Adela, misinterpreting the tone of his voice, sprang to her feet. 'Nay, Saxon! Please—do not hurt her. The knife is here——' She turned and pulled the pelts away, picked up the little weapon and held it out to him.

As he moved to take it, however, she drew back and said quietly, 'Give me your word that Frida will not be punished.'

His grim expression dissolved into a smile. 'And what, pray, do you think to do with *that*?' He held out his hand and took a step towards her.

There was a strange, fluttering sensation in her stomach and she was trembling slightly, but she drew up her arm sharply, threatening him with the knife. 'Give me your word!' As if, she thought ruefully, she could trust the word of such a man anyway.

He merely laughed. Crossing the room in a few strides, he took the knife from her, thrust it into his belt, and wrenching her arms behind her back, crushed her against him. He was just as savage and just as brutal when he kissed her this time as he had been a few minutes before in the hall. Furious, burning with anger and resentment and humiliation that could find no outlet, she was as rigid and unyielding in his arms as stone, and he was as impervious to the fact as he had been to her struggles.

But suddenly, something inside her sprang to life, a flame that flared, blazed intensely for the briefest moment, then flickered and died away slowly.

He released her, and in a blind, red rage that swept away every reasonable thought, her arm flew up and she slapped his face with all the force her angry young body could summon.

In an instant, his mouth claimed hers again, hungrily, relentlessly. She felt suddenly weak, and had no strength either to struggle, or even to brace herself against him, and stood limp and unresisting, finally aware of the futility of fighting him. A little whimper, half of pain, half of protest, escaped her, and immediately he relaxed the tight grip his fingers had on her arms, his mouth softening on hers and his kiss becoming a seductive caress.

A warmth began to steal slowly through her; she seemed unable to control her senses and her will was not her own. She found herself responding to the gentle, insistent persuasion of his kiss.

An agonised cry came out strangled and desperate as she suddenly twisted her head aside and wrenched herself free of his grasp, sinking, weak-kneed and shaking, on to the bed.

Unconsciously, she tensed herself for the sound of his mocking laughter, but it did not come and when she looked up to meet his gaze, there was no gleaming amusement in his eyes.

'You had best learn to have some respect for me, I think,' he said softly, moving to the door, 'for I begin to enjoy these little punishments. . . .'

For once, no answering quip sprang readily to her lips and she sat silently, eyes downcast and fists clenched, trying to gather her scattered senses. But when she heard him open the door, she looked up quickly: 'Frida——?' she whispered tentatively.

He shook his head a little, marvelling. 'Do you never give in, wench?' A smile lit his eyes. 'She was grateful to you for frequently saving her from the wrath of the Lady Marguerite. I had no intention of punishing her for that, merely to warn her what will happen if she is foolish enough to try to aid you again. That I will still do. As for this——' he tapped the hilt of the knife in his belt, 'I was well aware that you had it still. I am not completely a fool.'

A rush of uncontrollable fury suddenly overwhelmed her and with a cry she threw herself at him, arms raised and fists clenched, but she forgot the rope around her ankles and would have crashed, sprawling, to the floor but for the strong arms that reached out and caught her.

'Let me go! I hate you!' she screamed, beating uselessly at his chest. 'You nameless cur! How dare you trick me like that? You barbarian! You—you——' There was no word within her vocabulary descriptive enough. 'You—*Saxon*!' She spat the word out as though she despised everything it stood for.

He pushed her away and held her from him until the tempest in her had spent itself. She did not notice the gravity that had replaced the amusement in his blue eyes.

'Nay, wench,' he said quietly, 'do not hate me yet. You will have cause enough for that before this thing is done.'

Now what did that mean? The words seemed to linger even after he had released her and left the room, and she moved wearily back to her bed and lay down upon it, feeling sick with the turmoil of emotions going through her. She hated him for his arrogant, brutal treatment of her, for making such a fool of her and humiliating her in front of so many of the Saxons in the hall. And all the while he had no intention of punishing Frida!

Had she really felt the beginnings of response to his kiss? Perhaps she had imagined it? But she knew she had not. A wave of shame brought a warm blush to her cheeks and she turned over to bury her face in the soft pelts.

Oh, if only Sir Edward would hurry and get them out of this mess. Oh, for Guy's safe, undemanding arms about her. He has kissed her once, a gentle, tender kiss stolen one day when the gallery at Erinwald was deserted, which now seemed so chaste and loving compared to the ravaging of her mouth that Leowulf's had been.

Confused and disturbed, and angry both with herself and with him, she barely noticed the food she ate and when, later, she settled down to sleep, she passed a restless, dream-filled night.

Early next morning, she was roused by the sounds of commotion and raised voices outside, and moments later was roughly shaken awake by a girl as fair as she herself was dark, with long, flaxen hair hanging in two braids and wide blue eyes. 'You must hurry and make yourself ready,' she said, moving to the end of the bed and cutting the rope that tied Adela to it. 'Dermott is returning and my lord is waiting.'

'Waiting?' Adela queried as she rose. 'For what?'

'To meet with Sir Edward de Lise, of course. Dermott has made the arrangements. Please hurry.'

She went away, leaving Adela to dress and to

wonder at her identity. She could not remember having seen her at Erinwald, and as far as she knew Leowulf had taken only men with him when he had left for the hills, though others had joined him since then, and perhaps she had come with one of them.

She combed her sleep-tousled hair until it shone tangle-free down her back, but she had no time to braid it, for Leowulf's roar of 'Edith! What keeps you, girl?', echoing through the hall, brought the girl hurrying in, and Adela, sweeping her hair over one shoulder, followed her out of the room and along to the hall to join Marguerite, who was standing looking bemused at the activity around her.

Leowulf stood talking with Olwyn and a dishevelled person Adela guessed was Dermott, and he looked quite magnificent. Even she had to admit that. Over his tunic he wore a sheepskin, seeming to be carelessly flung over one shoulder and secured by his belt, into which was thrust a sword and the heavy, long-bladed knife Saxons called a 'seax'. Soft-skin, fleecelined boots clad his feet, leather thongs crossed up his legs over the hose he wore, and he carried a brown mantle over one arm.

Despite herself, her blood quickened at the sight of him. Such a man must surely turn the heart of any Saxon maid. The thought caused her to glance at the girl beside her, and the light shining in Edith's eyes as she, too, looked at Leowulf, gave Adela a little jolt. But the light was quenched instantly when he turned from his conversation and walked over to them.

''Tis bitter cold outside, Edith. They will need their mantles.'

'Yea, my lord,' she murmured, and went to fetch them.

Ignoring Marguerite, he turned his gaze on Adela, lingering on the shining mass of hair draped over her shoulder. 'We go to meet your uncle,' he said, returning his gaze to her face.

She had half expected him to look at her in that peculiarly mocking, half-amused way he had, or made some taunting comment about their confrontation the previous evening. However, he obviously had more important matters on his mind, and she resolutely thrust the whole incident out of her thoughts, at least for the present.

Remembering vividly the ride from Erin-wald, she looked up at him and said hopefully, 'May we have horses? I have no great desire to repeat the ordeal of last time.'

'I am sorry if you found my arms less than comfortable, wench,' he said solemnly. ''Tis not a complaint I receive very often!'

She ignored that. 'You have my word we will not try to escape,' she said, and added with an impulsive smile, 'At least, not until we meet Sir Edward!'

An answering smile tugged at the corner of his mouth, but his eyes narrowed slightly as he searched her face. For a long moment she met his penetrating gaze steadily, before he sighed and shook his head. 'Nay, I dare not trust you, little one. But it will not be so rough a ride for you this time—Dermott has arranged with de Lise that we meet where the forest road crosses the river. Besides,' he added with a faint smile, 'I would not deny myself the pleasure of holding you so close!'

He turned away before she could snap out a retort, and Marguerite whispered: 'I wish you would speak French, Adela! What is it? We are going to meet Edward, I suppose?'

Adela nodded briefly and translated the conversation. Then, as Edith returned, gave them the mantles and walked away, she added thoughtfully: 'Who is she, I wonder?'

Marguerite shrugged. 'What does it matter? We will soon be done with them all.'

But not, Adela thought, until my lord Leowulf has what he wants, and perhaps not even then....

When, a few minutes later, they were ready to leave, Leowulf took Adela up on his grey horse and instructed a brawny Saxon called Aelfric to take Marguerite. Olwyn stayed behind with about a third of the men to protect the women and children, but it was still a considerable show of Saxon strength that had assembled as the sun spread its watery winter light over the hilly horizon to set the frosty ground sparkling. A score of men, a party of Saxon horsemen that had too much the look of aggression and Adela, whilst appreciating the reason for it, wondered if it were quite wise.

'Put your arm around me,' Leowulf told her.

She looked up at him and shook her head. 'I shall be well enough.'

He merely shrugged and did not insist, but when they were ready to leave, he caused the horse to move off so suddenly that the jolt nearly unseated her. She glared at him, but slipped her arm round him, clutching his belt at the back and loosely entwining the fingers of her other hand in the horse's mane.

He held the reins easily, his left arm supporting her back and his right lying carelessly across her legs. She had to acknowledge that she was comfortable, but she was also acutely aware of his nearness.

She cast a surreptitious glance at the Saxon and wondered, not for the first time, why he seemed to treat her as the more important of his hostages. For the most part he ignored Marguerite, consigning her to the care of lesser men, when surely as Sir Edward's wife she ensured his co-operation far more than would a mere niece.

As she looked at him, she was conscious of a tautness about him, an inner tension that she could only attribute to the approaching meeting with her uncle and the audience with the King he hoped would eventually follow. Obviously it all meant a great deal to him.

She wondered why she so instinctively

LADY IN THE LION'S DEN 49

believed he was in earnest and that this was not all some elaborate ruse for a more sinister end. But she did believe him, and found herself hoping that the King would believe him also, enough to allow him to return to Erinwald as he wished.

She had a vague notion she should feel guilty at wanting him to succeed—Marguerite would doubtless be horrified to know of her sympathy with the Saxon.

Yet what would it matter to her, Adela, if the King looked favourably on Leowulf? They would have to quit Erinwald, of course, but William would no doubt give them other lands, and if she must live in England one manor was surely very much akin to another, and one lot of Saxon serfs much as any other. What did it matter to her? She would marry Guy and go back to Normandy.

She was surprised at the feeling of regret that came over her at the thought of leaving Erinwald. Had she grown so fond of it? So fond of Frida and Cedric and Edwina and the others?

Well, perhaps it was only natural. She had lived amongst them for the better part of a year, and because her uncle was always so busy and Marguerite made no attempt to learn the language, the burden of domestic problems and organisation fell on her shoulders and brought her much closer to the Saxon people there.

She wondered if Leowulf, who had said that

there was little he did not know about what had been happening at Erinwald, knew of Marguerite's meagre contribution to the running of the manor. Perhaps that was why he treated her as he did.

'Do you like what you see, wench?' His voice, though soft, startled her into realising that she had been staring at him, and in some confusion she avoided his eyes. 'How a man looks does not always reflect what he is,' she said coldly.

'Oh, such wisdom from such a slip of a wench!' There was an edge to his voice which caused her to turn her head a little to look at him. He raised an eyebrow. 'You do not like what you think I am.' It was more a statement than a question.

'Do you censure me for that?' she demanded. 'You have scarce endeared yourself to me!'

Yesterday he would merely have laughed at her, caring nothing. But now there was only a barely perceptible tightening of a muscle beneath the scratches Marguerite had made, and a slight hardening in his eyes that she might have imagined, to indicate that he had even heard her. It made her slightly uneasy. His arrogant jibes and mockery were one thing, but this tension that was so marked in him this morning seemed uncharacteristic.

However, as he was obviously in no humour for conversation, she was unlikely to discover what else troubled him, and with a faint sigh resolutely thrust the Saxon and his problems out of her mind, turning instead to the less unsettling prospect of seeing her uncle and Guy.

The place arranged for the meeting was, Adela guessed, about halfway to Erinwald, a meadow where the rough forest road forded a wide but shallow stream. As they approached, she realised why the Saxon had brought most of his men, for Sir Edward stood grim-faced at his horse's head, and behind him his entire entourage, still mounted, were drawn up in three ranks, looking almost prepared for battle, and as hostile as Leowulf had evidently known they would be.

The four of them, Aelfric and Marguerite, Leowulf and herself, dismounted and walked towards Sir Edward. A few feet away they halted and Leowulf moved a pace ahead. The breath of men and horses alike rose in steamy clouds on the frosty air.

Adela had never seen her uncle look so angry, but his first words were an anxious enquiry as to their well-being. 'We have been well treated, uncle,' she said quickly, fearing that with her husband so close, Marguerite might say something the Saxon would make her regret later.

With a long look, and a brief nod, Sir Edward turned to Leowulf and curtly demanded an explanation for his outrageous actions.

Leowulf, speaking French, began by apologising that such measures had been necessary, and gave his assurance that no harm would come to either lady. Then he went on to relate his proposals for the King as he had described them to Adela the day before, and asked that Sir Edward request William to see him.

'There is one thing more I would have you discuss with William,' he went on and then paused for a moment. 'I wish to wed the Lady Adela.'

There was a shocked silence. Adela gasped, her face suffused with colour, and then slowly drained, leaving her white and shaken. Marguerite's hand closed on her arm, and there were angry murmurs and oaths from the Norman contingent.

'*You*—wish to——' Sir Edward seemed to choke on the words.

'Yes,' Leowulf said calmly. 'I am told William favours such marriages, for there is no better way to unite Norman and Saxon. 'Tis a measure of my sincerity and will ensure my loyalty to William.'

Adela, only her pride preventing her unleashing her enraged temper on the Saxon, stood trembling with anger, staring straight ahead of her, bright-eyed and tight-lipped, her fists clenched tightly at her sides and her head held high.

Guy de Brec did not possess such control. He

leapt from his horse, drew his sword and flung himself towards Leowulf, but as instinctively as the Saxon reached for his seax, two Normans sprang forward and dragged Guy back. Sir Edward turned and said a few sharp words under his breath which stilled the struggling young man instantly.

Adela slowly released the sharp breath she had drawn, conscious of a great relief—she did not want this meeting to turn into a bloody battle because of her.

There was a little more discussion before the two groups parted. Sir Edward had three days to see the King and return with an answer. And if he did not....

The threat was left unspoken.

CHAPTER
FOUR

THE return journey was an ordeal for Adela. Held once again in Leowulf's arms, she kept her head turned and her eyes on the road in front, aware that her loose hair was frequently caught up by the wind and flicked back in his face. She hoped it annoyed him.

Too angry and confused to make any sense out of the turmoil of her thoughts, she clung to the conviction that neither her uncle nor the King would contemplate a marriage between the Lady Adela de Lise and a Saxon barbarian whose reputation for violence and wenching was well known.

She was appalled, furious and humiliated, and spoke not a single word all the way back, nor relaxed her rigid bearing. Leowulf was equally silent, and forced a relentless pace which he did not slacken until the low buildings of his retreat came into view.

Olwyn was emerging from one of the outbuildings as they rode in and he came up with a cheerful greeting as Adela, without waiting for Leowulf to help her down, slipped easily to the ground and walked quickly past the surprised Olwyn into the hall.

'What ails the wench?' he demanded, frowning as he noticed Marguerite's stony countenance and the expressive look Aelfric cast his way as he led her inside.

Leowulf did not answer immediately, but dismounted and put his hand on Olwyn's shoulder as they followed them in. 'She is something upset, I think, that I told her uncle I wished to wed her.'

Olwyn stopped in mid-stride and swung round. '*What*?' Disbelief registered on his face; then, with a half-smile, he said, 'You jest.'

Leowulf shook his head. 'Nay, my friend. I do not jest.'

For a moment Olwyn seemed stupefied, unable to accept what his ears had heard. Others in the hall had also stopped what they were doing to cast startled glances at their lord. 'Then you are mad!' he exploded. 'What devilry possessed you? I have known you since we were stripling lads together, and never known your wits so addled! Are you suddenly turned fool, man? You make a mockery of it all with such a demand. William will never agree now! He'll not have a want-wit swearing fealty to him!'

Leowulf laid a hand on his arm. His face was set, his eyes hard and glinting and his voice low and controlled. 'Have a care, Olwyn, my friend. I am in earnest over this and no man—nay, not even you—shall call me a fool for it. I will have that wench to wife.'

'And endanger us all for it!' With a sound of disgust, Olwyn swung away, checking slightly when he caught sight of Adela watching them. Then he strode angrily across the hall and disappeared through the doorway that led to the kitchens.

Leowulf, with a face like stone, walked across to the two girls and jerked his head towards the second of the doorways. 'Come.'

' 'Tis too much to expect, no doubt,' Adela said coldly, 'that you will grant me the courtesy of an explanation.'

'You have heard my reasons.'

'Yea, and have only contempt for them!' she retorted scornfully. Then, her voice heavy with sarcasm, she went on, 'I will not be a hostage for your safety, my brave lord Leowulf, and if you believe that my uncle and the King will ever agree to a marriage between us, you are mad indeed!'

'I am in no humour to exchange pleasantries with you, wench!' he caught her arm. 'And if you value your safety,' he added in a dangerous voice, 'you would do well to obey me. Come.'

She pulled back, daring to defy him. 'Merely because Olwyn had courage enough to tell you he thinks you are a fool, is no reason to break my arm!' She wrenched free of his grasp. 'Do you intend to keep us confined to those chambers for three days? A fine way to treat the lady you profess to wish to wed!'

For a moment his face was inscrutable. Then,

grudgingly, he replied, 'Very well. Escape is impossible without help and no one will aid you now. So you may have the freedom of this building, but you are not to go outside.'

She met his gaze and inclined her head. 'Thank you,' she said tautly. 'You are very kind!' He sent her a withering look, turned on his heel and went back after Olwyn.

Thus left, both girls felt somewhat at a loss. The Saxons had returned to their various tasks, discussing the morning's revelations in hushed tones, and there seemed little they could do but shed their mantles and sit down on one of the benches at the long table.

Adela was still incensed by Leowulf's treatment of her and leaned her elbows on the table and rested her chin in her cupped hands. 'How dare he, Margo?' she demanded in a low voice. 'Does he think I am a mere serf to be bartered away at a man's whim? A piece of merchandise?'

'If he thinks that,' Marguerite said quietly, 'he will soon discover his mistake! 'Tis as well, I think, that he will not hear what Edward says about him to the King!'

Adela turned to look at her, realising for the first time that her uncle would view the situation very differently from herself. Only this morning she had been hoping Leowulf would succeed in his aims and be restored to Erinwald as a loyal subject of William, sympathising with his cause. But her uncle . . . He would see a man who, by his deeds this past year, had brought to the king's attention the fact that Sir Edward de Lise had not really fully succeeded in doing what he had been sent to Erinwald to do. Moreover, Leowulf had taken advantage of his absence to abduct his wife and niece, and then had made demands of the king, using him as a mediator. . . .

She could well imagine how bad her uncle could—and no doubt would—make it all seem. Suppose the King were moved to act against Leowulf? A flutter of unease stirred in the pit of her stomach at the several disagreeable possibilities that suggested themselves. 'Oh, Margo,' she murmured, 'however will it all come right?'

Marguerite sighed and smiled a little. 'Edward will find a way.'

Adela could only marvel at her confidence. But then, of course, her idea of a happy conclusion to all this was quite different from Marguerite's. She did not want anyone to suffer unduly, whereas Marguerite would doubtless quite cheerfully see Leowulf hang.

Hating the boredom of having nothing to do, and needing something to keep her from thinking too much about Leowulf and what might happen when her uncle returned from seeing the King, Adela let her gaze stray to the several Saxon women seated by the fire and working at a very fine tapestry, which was presumably intended for Erinwald.

Perhaps, she mused, if they were both quiet and untroublesome and friendly towards everyone, the Saxons might grow careless in their watching, might trust them too far. Then, perhaps tomorrow, there might come a chance to escape. For although she did not believe that the King would even consider agreeing to Leowulf marrying her, Adela realised that it was possible he would agree to grant him an audience, and the Saxon was likely to keep them hostage for as long as it suited him.

At first the Saxon women were unwilling to allow the Norman ladies to join them, and much of their reluctance seemed to be directed towards Marguerite—she had not made herself popular with the Saxons during Sir Edward's absence from Erinwald. But they overcame their reticence when Frida pointed out that both ladies were skilled at such things, and with two more needles working, it would be finished all the sooner.

Marguerite made herself much more amiable than Adela had seen her with Saxons for some time, and she even attempted a few words of their language. She herself, however, was restless, and although she worked on a corner of the tapestry for some time, she soon tired of it, and murmuring a few words of excuse, she sent Marguerite a smiling look to encourage her to continue, and rose from the little circle.

As she turned away, she saw Olwyn standing

in the doorway surveying the world outside, and she walked along beside the table and sat down at the end of the bench only a few feet from him. He turned and looked at her, and to her relief there was little of the hostility about him that there had been earlier.

He nodded towards the women by the fire. 'The stitchery does not interest you?'

She shrugged. 'Yes, well enough. But not today.' She paused and then raised her troubled eyes to his. 'Olwyn, why did he do it?'

He made a sound of disgust. 'There can only be one reason, but I like it not.'

She nodded and could not prevent the trace of bitterness in her voice. 'He wishes to wed me to secure his position with William, and as a hostage to ensure that the King will not attack once he is back at Erinwald!'

Olwyn looked at her sharply and narrowed his eyes. For a moment he said nothing, then: ''Tis madness, all of it. He has no right to do this to you.'

'Surely you do not believe the King will agree, too!'

Olwyn shrugged. 'Leowulf is used to having what he wants.'

This ambiguous statement did not seem to be an answer, and it rendered Adela silent, powerless to quell the sudden fluttering in her stomach. 'But,' she began tentatively, 'you do not have to be as guilty as he. You could, perhaps . . . help us. To—to get away. . . .?' Her heart sank, aware even as she spoke of the futility of such a clumsy plea.

He smiled a little, almost regretfully. 'Nay. I owe him some loyalty. Indeed, I owe him my life.' He returned his gaze to the activity outside, and beckoned her. 'Look.' She rose, mystified, and went to stand beside him. 'I am not so brave, either,' he said with a wry smile, 'that I would make an enemy of such a man as that.'

The sight that met her eyes as she followed his gaze made her blood run cold.

Leowulf was standing with a handful of his men, and he was practising with an axe that glinted in the late-afternoon sunlight; the type of axe which had caused such havoc amongst the Normans at the time of the invasion, severing horses' heads and men's limbs at a single blow. He stood half-turned away from her, legs set apart, the axe held in both hands, blade down, in front of him. Slowly he lifted it and swung it to the left, then over his shoulder, the muscles of his arms hardening to take the weight as he raised the heavy, deadly weapon high over his head.

Suddenly, for a few terrible moments, Adela could visualise him at Hastings; she could hear the sounds of battle, the shouting and screaming and the clash of metal. She could see her father on his knees before him, the sudden horror of realisation in his eyes. The axe paused in mid-air for the briefest instant, and then, with all the force of hatred, it crashed downwards....

She screamed. Her head reeled, the world swam and she pressed her fingers to her eyes to block out the nightmare. Vaguely she heard a voice close to her, felt a hand on her arm and a hand gripping her shoulder; but she fought him off, twisted away and ran across the hall, sweeping aside the heavy curtain and half-stumbling into the bedchamber, pushing the door closed behind her.

Dropping to her knees before the fire, she buried her face in her hands and the tears that squeezed beneath her lashes fell silently through her fingers. They were few, for tears did not come easily to Adela, and she quickly brushed them away at the sound of raised voices outside.

A moment later the door opened and she turned her head, half-expecting Marguerite, but it was Leowulf. 'What ails you?' When she made no reply and turned deliberately back to face the fire, he crossed the room in a few strides and firmly, but not unkindly, raised her to her feet and turned her round to face him.

She pulled violently away. 'Don't touch me! Can you not leave me in peace? Go away!'

He shook his head, frowning a little. 'Nay. Why did you cry out? Was it Olwyn? Did he——?'

'He did nothing! 'Tis you. I hate you, you

murdering swine, I hate you and I hate this accursed country, do you hear me?'

'Yea, I hear you, for you scream like a common beggar-woman——' It was an exaggeration, and if it was designed to anger her further, it succeeded. But he easily caught the arm that flew up to strike him and he held it firmly as his free hand closed around her other wrist. 'Why do you hate me so suddenly?'

'I have cause enough to hate you, I think!'

'Yea, but no more now than you had a few hours ago, and you were not so distraught then.'

'It might have been you killed my father! *You* who cut him down as if he were no more than a log of wood. You, with your m-mighty axe that clove him in—in two....' Her voice trembled and broke, and she half-turned away.

He was silent for a moment, and then released his hold on her. 'And for that—possibility,' he said softly, emphasising the word slightly, 'you would hate me and all my kind? Nay, wench. 'Tis not in you. You have proved that all these past months at Erinwald. 'Tis merely the injustice that angers you, I think.'

He reached out and lifted her chin so that she was forced to look at him, and with his other hand he brushed several strands of hair from her face. 'I killed many men that day,' he said quietly. ''Tis possible one was your father. But 'tis also possible it was your father's sword—or your uncle's—that slew my brother Wilnoth.'

She could only look at him in sudden dismay. She had not even known he had a brother, and somehow that seemed to heighten her guilt.

'I will send the Lady Marguerite to you,' he growled as he turned away and went to the door.

'Oh, no, please!' The last thing she wanted at that moment was Marguerite fussing over her. She wanted to apologise, to beg his forgiveness for her selfish outburst, to tell him that she knew how greatly the Saxons had suffered, and how many of those here had the loss of kin to grieve ... but the words would not come, only unshed tears that glistened in her eyes. 'I—I will come in a little while,' she managed to say. He looked at her intently for a moment, then nodded briefly and left her, closing the door behind him.

She did not know how long it was that she stood there, resenting him, condemning herself for allowing him to upset her, and trying to find some justification for the violent way she had reacted. Not knowing that he had a brother killed at Hastings was no excuse, she knew, for the things she had said to him.

Without realising what she was doing, she moved to the chest to pick up the bone comb that lay there and began drawing it through her hair, endeavouring to restore some order to the confusion of her thoughts and regain some of the composure that had been completely destroyed in the last few minutes.

By the time she returned to the hall, it had grown gloomy and the torches were lit. There was no sign of Leowulf, but Marguerite sat by the fire and she looked up with a mixture of relief and anxiety when Adela sat down beside her.

'It was nothing serious, Margo,' she said in answer to her unspoken query. 'Leowulf had an axe. For a moment I thought I could see him slaying father with it. . . .' The bland words conveyed nothing of the horror of that moment, but Marguerite could see that she was upset, and, anxious to divert her thoughts to pleasanter subjects, talked of persuading Sir Edward to take them to London when all this was over.

Adela was far too concerned with the present, however, to be able to do more than smile vaguely and agree that it would be an enjoyable diversion.

The evening meal was prepared and set upon the table, and the men called from their various pursuits. Leowulf came in with Edith, and he was evidently in a much improved mood. His arm rested easily across her shoulders and he was laughing heartily—much to the girl's apparent embarrassment, for she was blushing furiously and held her eyes downcast, despite the smile that hovered round her mouth.

Adela looked away, wondering how the girl felt about her lord's wish to wed a Norman maid—although no doubt Leowulf's pleasures would not be overly restricted by the inconvenience of a wife!

As everyone sat down at the table, he strode across to his two captives and took an arm of each. 'Come,' he said. 'Are you not hungry?'

Adela would have preferred to eat alone in her chamber, and seeing her obvious reluctance, he smiled and patted her arm reassuringly. 'You must grow used to sitting beside me, little one. As my wife, it will be expected of you!'

She gritted her teeth. She refused to create another scene in front of the Saxons for Leowulf's entertainment! He bade them sit one on either side of him and seemed in a very jovial humour—evidently he had resolved his differences with Olwyn, and Edith, it seemed, had succeeded in raising his spirits quite considerably!

Adela found that her appetite had deserted her. She ate little and said nothing, aware of his gaze upon her from time to time but declining to look at him for fear of encountering that mocking amusement, and losing her temper again.

The men did not appear unduly concerned over the new element in Leowulf's plans, and it seemed that if he wished to take a Norman wench to wife that was entirely his affair. If they did object, or dislike the idea, they did so silently. Indeed, Olwyn's was the only dissenting voice she had heard, and that had been quickly stilled.

She could not help but wonder what it was about Leowulf that bound men like these to him with such loyalty. They had followed him from Erinwald, or joined him since, to continue to fight their Norman conquerors, and they remained with him when he decided to give up and throw in his lot with William. At a word from him, the others—those who had been at Erinwald this past year—abandoned everything and followed him to a future that was, at best, uncertain, not knowing whether or not they would ever see their homes again.

She was uncomfortably aware that she, too, was in his power, that *her* future was also in his hands, whatever the King decided. She could not shake off the disturbing conviction that it was not going to come to the swift and happy conclusion it should.

It was in this thoughtful, troubled mood that Adela endured the meal, and when it was over and Leowulf allowed them to retire, it stayed with her. She and Marguerite were to spend the night in separate chambers again, presumably because they were less troublesome apart than they were together, but it was an extravagance in the overcrowded conditions of the settlement. A man stood guard at the curtain, and there would doubtless be someone there all night.

Adela was not, however, entirely sorry for

her solitude. It had been a long, wearying day and she ached from the strain of it. She removed most of her clothes and left them in a pile on the floor, before sliding beneath the soft warmth of the pelts and closing her eyes with a sigh.

CHAPTER
FIVE

SURPRISINGLY, after the events of the day, Adela slipped easily into a deep, dreamless sleep from which she did not wake until well after sunrise. For a while she lay floating in the half-realms, too sleepy to think and merely drowsing in the soft warmth of the pelts; but her contentment was short-lived as memories of the previous day awakened in her mind with disturbing clarity.

She groaned and turned on to her side, feeling for a moment totally incapable of dealing with the situation with any degree of strength and pride. The two days between now and her uncle's return from the King would be long and stressful, and she was afraid of what Leowulf might do when his ambitions were thwarted.

However, she forced herself to rise, and with the water which had been brought in at some time while she slept, she washed and refreshed herself, and dressed slowly. There seemed no need to hasten. It was a very cold morning so she wrapped her mantle around her before leaving the room and, completely ignoring the suspicious looks of the man on guard outside,

opened the door of Marguerite's chamber and
peeped inside. Marguerite was still asleep, so
she closed the door again quietly and went on
into the hall.

Frida came forward and bade her be seated
while she fetched some food, but Adela, who
had no more appetite this morning than she
had had last night, shook her head.

'But you ate little yesterday, my lady,' the
Saxon girl protested. 'You should eat something.'

'I want nothing, Frida, thank you.'

'But——'

Adela silenced her with a look and turned
away towards the fire, where one of the young
children was loudly demanding attention. As
Marguerite did not emerge from her chamber,
Adela was quite content to amuse herself playing with young Ewen for a while, for there was
little else she could do.

It was snowing heavily outside, and when
several of the children clamoured to be allowed
out to play in it, she was pleased to help dress
them warmly, and then stood in the doorway
clutching Ewen's hand and watching them with
a faint smile playing round her mouth. Snow
had always fascinated her, and to see the land
lying in hushed tranquillity and covered in a
glistening whiteness filled her with a strange
mixture of joy and humility.

Ewen tugged on her arm, and with a soft
laugh she allowed him to pull her outside,

forgetting Leowulf's command that they were not to go beyond the confines of the building. With a gurgle of delight, Ewen pulled gleefully away from her and hurled himself into the mêlée of young limbs and flying snow.

The women, keeping watchful eyes on their offspring, were turned away from her, and across by one of the outbuildings Leowulf and several other men were preoccupied with the examination of a horse which appeared to have hurt its leg and was dancing skittishly about, extremely nervous in the swirling whiteness. None, it seemed, had noticed her.

As Adela realised this, she hesitated for only a moment before turning and walking quickly towards the trees, a confusion of thoughts chasing themselves through her mind. It was simple. Simple to run through the woods away from this place; one person on foot was much more difficult to follow than two on horseback and she could hide herself easily; with a little luck she would encounter a Norman patrol before she had gone more than a few miles. A brief glance back told her that no one had noticed her walking away and she started to run, ducking beneath low branches and weaving between the black trunks that showed so starkly against the whiteness.

However, her feet slowed as the snow that had fallen on her from the trees melted and soaked through her mantle and gown to numb her skin with coldness and restore a little

reason. She came to a halt and stood shivering.
Her wits were surely addled. It was impossible,
of course. She had no food, no knife to protect
herself from the wild animals, no more than a
mantle against the weather, and in such conditions it was unlikely the Norman patrols
would venture so far into the hills. She would
freeze to death before she came anywhere
near an inhabited place, let alone as far as
Erinwald.

Whatever Leowulf was, he was scarcely so
terrifying that she would die rather than
stay two days as his 'guest'. And what of
Marguerite? Had she grown so callous that
she would attempt to escape herself and leave
Marguerite—her aunt and her friend—to
whatever fate was in store? To face Leowulf's
wrath?

She knew she was not so selfish. Slowly, she
turned and began to walk back, and when she
reached the edge of the trees, she walked along
a little further so that she emerged into the
open at the side of the building, out of view of
the people in front of it.

As she turned the corner and walked
towards the door, there was a terrified whinny
from the horse with an injured leg and he
reared up, hooves flailing, and plunged down,
breaking free of his captors. In the same instant
little Ewen, who had been playing by himself
some distance from the others, saw Adela and
began running towards her. In his excitement,

he did not even hear her horrified cry of warning.

Vaguely she was aware of Leowulf and the other men running, of women snatching children out of danger. But Ewen was oblivious, and the smile on his little face seemed to lend wings to her feet. Adela flew across the ground, panic driving all conscious thought from her mind, and her ears filled with the sound of pounding hooves.

She reached him seconds before the horse, but just as she stretched out to scoop him up, she tripped and fell. On her knees, she half-pushed, half threw him back towards Leowulf with a force lent by desperation. But then, as she tried to twist herself away, one of the horse's hooves caught the side of her head and the glancing blow sent her sprawling, with a shaft of pain splitting through her head, into a crumpled heap. With a half-gasp, she sank into black oblivion....

It seemed as though only a few seconds had passed before the misty blackness began to clear and Adela became aware of the throbbing in her head, of strong arms that were holding her, and muffled voices through the fog clouding her senses. She struggled to move, but had little strength and could not even force her eyes open. As she stirred, the arms that held her gripped her a little more firmly and a familiar voice bade her lie still, and despite her discomfort and throbbing head, a warmth stole over her and she relaxed against him.

Someone was bathing the side of her head with cool water, and a goblet of hot, fragrant liquid was being held to her lips while a familiar, female voice told her to drink. Obediently she sipped it, its bitter sweetness making her grimace in distaste, but after a few moments her head cleared and she forced her eyes to open to find herself looking at Frida, who smiled a little with compassion in her eyes.

Shifting her gaze upwards to Leowulf's face, she encountered blue eyes full of concern. She avoided them for the disquiet they caused, and glanced about her; they were in the bedchamber she had occupied earlier, and a heavy quiet seemed to settle over everything.

A sharp anxiety over Ewen seized her, and she half rose, but sank back with a gasp as a wave of nausea washed over her.

'Lie still, little fool,' the Saxon chided gently, and then, as if guessing the reason for her panic, added: 'Ewen is safe and unharmed. But we will talk of it later. By some miracle you were not killed, but your head has taken a mighty blow and you must rest.' He lowered her gently on to the bed and put her hand to the cloth he held over the wound. 'Hold this—it bleeds slightly still.' He pulled the wolf pelts over her. 'Frida will sit with you. Try to sleep.'

He departed, leaving Frida to take up her

stitchery and retreat to the chair by the fire. Adela eased her throbbing head to a more comfortable position and closed her eyes.

Of the rest of the day she knew little, vaguely aware from time to time of hushed voices and someone quietly moving about in the room, and occasionally she was lifted and made to sip some of that pungent brew. But it all seemed to be happening through a mist, and it was some time before her head ceased to throb so violently and she was able to sleep a little.

When, finally, she came fully to her senses, the room was almost in darkness, lightened only by the glow of the fire, and Frida was gone. Gingerly she sat up and pushed aside the pelts, waiting for the throbbing in her head to return; but it seemed to have gone and she swung her legs down and stood up. Splashing some water on her face and drawing the comb gingerly through her hair, careful to avoid the healing wound, she straightened her clothing and stood for a moment, listening. The place was unnaturally quiet, and she was conscious of a little stab of anxiety. Perhaps something dreadful had happened. Perhaps after all, Ewen *had* been harmed.

She left the room and went to the door of the adjacent chamber; Marguerite was not there and she went on to the hall. A low murmur of voices greeted her as she pulled aside the curtain and found everyone already at the evening meal. Her eyes sought Marguerite, and she smiled at the look of relief that flooded the elder girl's face.

Leowulf rose instantly from his place between Olwyn and Edith and came towards her. 'You should not be up,' he said severely. 'Return to the chamber and I will have food brought in to you.'

She shook her head. 'I am well enough. My headache is almost gone.'

He sent her a searching look and then nodded. 'Very well then. Come. Sit with us and eat. There is fresh-caught meat and——'

'I thank you,' she said coolly, inclining her head, 'but I want nothing.'

He took her arm firmly to lead her towards the tables. 'You have had nothing all day and little enough yesterday. You must eat.'

'So that I may not fall ill and spoil your plans for me?' she asked sweetly. 'I am sorry, but the food here tastes bitter in my mouth.'

'It seems,' said the Saxon in a low tone, 'that the accident has neither sweetened your tongue nor put sense into your head. If you do not wish to be fed by force like a child, you will sit down and eat.'

Toying for a moment with the idea of telling him exactly what she thought of him, she fully realised that he was quite capable of carrying out his threat. She sighed heavily, allowing him instead to lead her to the table, where room was made for her next to Marguerite—and under the watchful eye of the Saxon himself.

Under his gaze, she forced herself to eat a little, though the food seemed tasteless to her and stuck in her throat so that she was compelled to drink more ale than was her custom. 'Why is it so quiet, Margo?' she asked softly in French. 'Leowulf told me that Ewen was unharmed, but——'

'Ewen is perfectly well,' Marguerite told her. 'But the Saxon has insisted on complete quiet in the hall since it happened, so that you might not be disturbed.'

Adela cast a swift glance towards Leowulf, who was laughing at some remark of Edith's. She looked away, quelling a pang of something uneasy as Marguerite went on: 'When he carried you inside and would not allow me near, I thought you had been killed. But then he said you were not badly hurt and were sleeping, and that I should sit with you. He was almost pleasant, and seemed more than a little concerned over you. Are you quite recovered?'

Adela reassured her, and as she turned her head suddenly and disconcertingly encountered Leowulf's intense blue gaze upon her. A strange sensation coursed through her veins, and she averted her eyes quickly, blushing. What was it about this Saxon that he could have such an effect on her?

She could eat no more, but made a pretence of nibbling at the meats, and it was with heartfelt relief that she rose from the table with the other women at the end of the meal.

Marguerite, who had spent the afternoon working on the tapestry, returned to it quite happily, leaving Adela reflecting wryly that however bad a situation, her aunt, despite her temper, could be made to tolerate it quietly enough if only she had a needle in her hand and a cloth to work upon. Even if that cloth was intended to hang at Erinwald after the de Lise family had been forced to leave.

Adela herself would have gone directly to her chamber but for Ewen's mother, who came up to her, eyes bright and shining with tears and gratitude, to grasp her hands and, dropping to her knees before her, thanked her in a voice choked with emotion for saving her son's life.

Taken completely unawares, and her head a little light because of the ale, Adela was momentarily nonplussed, but she recovered quickly and drew the woman to her feet. 'I did only what any other close enough would have done, Edwina.'

The woman shook her head, and glanced swiftly round before drawing the younger girl into the shadows of the doorway. 'Nay, mistress, you were quicker than many another would have been. But I have nothing to give you save——' She stopped, and lowered her voice. 'My lord has no right to keep you here thus, and if there is some way to help you, I will do it. Anything. It would not be difficult for me to——'

'No, Edwina,' Adela quietly but very firmly hushed her. 'I will not have you taking risks for us. We have only to wait for my uncle's return from the King to be freed from this lion's den.'

Shadows passed across the young woman's face. 'I fear for us when that happens, my lady,' she confessed in a trembling whisper. 'Sir Edward will want vengeance for this deed, and the King will not be easily appeased——'

'But 'tis not our way to punish the innocent, Edwina. I confess that when we were taken from Erinwald I was angry with you all for the way you repaid my uncle for his kindness towards you. But I know now that Leowulf is not a man to trifle with, and you would have had little choice. This I shall tell my uncle.'

Thus allaying the woman's fears, and acknowledging her expressions of gratitude with more than a little embarrassment, she escaped to her chamber thankfully. She felt cold and a little faint so she pulled the pelts off the bed, wrapped them around her and then prodded the fire into life before sitting huddled up in the chair beside its blazing warmth.

But her solitude was short-lived, for the door opened and when she glanced up and saw it was Leowulf, her heart gave an uncomfortable jolt, and she looked quickly away again. He came and stood before her. 'Do you feel unwell still?' he asked gently. 'You are pale.'

She moved her head in denial. 'I have a slight

headache, nothing more. Perhaps it would go if I were left to rest in peace!'

He chuckled. 'You would do as well to learn my humours before you sharpen that tongue on me, my sweet, for I am not always in a mood to tolerate such a cutting edge, and at such times would prefer a gentler maid.'

'I shall not be in your company long enough to learn anything about you, Saxon,' she retorted and half-turned away, presenting him with her shoulder and staring defiantly into the fire.

He reached down, took her arms and raised her to her feet, and she, light-headed from the ale and still shivering very slightly, was powerless to resist as a strange weakness washed over her at his touch.

His eyes, dark and intense in the firelight, searched hers as though looking for an answer to some question he was asking himself. 'I am a fool,' he said quietly on a heavy sigh, and more to himself than to her. 'It has been ill-done ...' He left the sentence unfinished and, drawing her slowly towards him, touched her lips very gently with his, and held her firmly as she tensed and tried to pull away. His kiss aroused all her senses and set her pulses racing, and she felt herself lean against him, felt her lips respond to his and could do nothing to prevent it.

Eventually, he pushed her gently away and held her at arm's length, and she, struggling to regain her composure, defied a strong desire to flee, and said caustically: 'You *were* a fool to add me to your terms, Saxon. Your people will not respect you any the more for such folly. You have stretched their loyalty enough already, I think. And I fear this stupidity will lose you your cause and William will have none of you. I, I began by sympathising with you and would perhaps have tried to help you. Now I have only contempt for you.'

He stared at her long and hard for some time, his thoughts impossible to guess. But then, in a quiet voice, he said, 'I am truly a fool, wench. But I think not for the reasons you believe.' He stopped, and after a moment, sighed heavily. 'Yea, but 'tis done now.'

'It can be undone.'

He shook his head. 'Nay. But perhaps it will yet come right.' With that, he dropped his arms and turned away, but then paused and looked back at her. 'Why did you come back when you ran into the woods? You had a chance of escape.'

She stared at him. 'You saw me, but you allowed me to go? Why?'

'You would not have gone far. I should have caught you easily.'

She was silent a moment, knowing the truth of it. 'I came back because it was a foolish thing to attempt, and because of Marguerite.'

Again, that long look that made her doubt the truth of her own words. He said nothing, merely nodded, and then turned and left her alone once more.

She was left, also, confused. Every confrontation with him seemed to reveal a different man, and her own feelings towards him were such a turmoil of hate, distrust, contempt, resentment and, somehow, a grudging admiration, that she was totally at a loss to know how to deal with him.

It was something that kept her awake that night, for she was unable to banish the disturbing sensations that thoughts of the Saxon aroused. The sooner she could return to her uncle, the happier she would feel. The sooner she and Guy married and returned to Normandy the better.

Even thoughts of Guy de Brec were not enough to soothe her, and eventually sheer exhaustion brought her sleep. But it was sleep disturbed by strange dreams of lions and Saxons and wedding feasts.

CHAPTER
SIX

THE morning was clear, cold and sparkling, the previous day's snow lying frozen and glittering frostily in the pale sunlight. Adela stood in the doorway silently appreciating the beauty of it, whilst at the same time cursing the snow. It had doubtless delayed her uncle, and she held few hopes of seeing him before tomorrow was halfway through. She glanced up at the cloudless winter-blue sky and prayed that the bad weather kept away, and did not delay him further.

She sighed and her gaze shifted to the tall, strong figure of Leowulf as he and some of his men prepared to go hunting. It was a pity, she thought, that she could no longer be in sympathy with him, for such a man deserved better than the furtive life he was leading in the hills.

She caught herself up in the thought, and blushed at it, and almost at the same moment, her heart gave a sudden lurch for he turned from his horse, caught her looking at him, and began to walk towards her. She turned in confusion and went quickly inside.

There she encountered the hostile gaze of

Edith, regarding her across the room with resentment glinting in the Saxon-blue of her eyes. Adela did not blame her for feeling resentful—it must be galling indeed to be in love with a man who calmly announces he wishes to wed another for no better reason than to secure his safety. But at the same time, she wished only to avoid her and walked through to the chamber she had been given which was in fact, Leowulf's own.'

There was no sanctuary for her there. Moments later, he came in and, giving her no more than a cursory glance, rummaged briefly in the coffer that stood at the foot of the bed and pulled out a heavy mantle. He straightened, and folding the garment across his arm stood for a moment regarding her. 'You flee from me, wench,' he said quietly. 'There is no need. I mean you no ill——'

'No ill?' she interrupted, and paused, forcing herself to keep her voice low. 'You would wed me, though. Is your conceit so great that you think that would do me no ill? 'Tis Guy de Brec I love and Guy I'll wed, and Guy who will return with me to Normandy.'

He shook his head. 'I have known you but a few days, little one, and yet already I know you better than you know yourself. Guy de Brec is a mere stripling lad—what does he know of love?' He moved forward and gripped her shoulder with his free hand, brushing away the long hair she had left loose, and, bending his head, he very gently kissed her neck just above her shoulder. The sensual gesture sent a shiver over her, but she did not pull away. His mouth moved to hers, and this time her response to his kiss was positive and unmistakable.

When he pushed her gently from him, she was instantly filled with shame and turned away, sinking on to the bed and willing him to go away. He did so, quietly, and she was left trying to answer a headful of seemingly unanswerable questions.

She could not be alone with the turmoil of her thoughts, however, for Marguerite wandered in a few minutes later, bored and petulant, and seated herself in the chair by the fire.

'That barbarian has gone off on his hunt, thank God,' she said on a weary sigh. 'But he has made certain he has left enough men that we cannot escape——' She broke off abruptly. 'How pale you are! What is it?'

The younger girl pulled herself together and smiled. ''Tis nothing. My head is still a little muzzy from the accident, that is all.'

'That accursed man!' she exclaimed. 'That horse should have been killed. And I should have thought Edward might have made some attempt to deliver us from this! How could he simply leave us here like this to suffer such indignities——?'

'Oh, Margo!' Adela, irritated, interrupted the complaint with less than her usual patience.

'He is gone to the King. How can he be in two places at once?'

'He has men, Adela. He did not have to abandon us for three days. And what of Guy? Surely you expected Guy to make some attempt to free us? The fondness between you is well known.'

'We do not know what is happening with them, Margo. It is useless to speculate. They are thinking of our safety and I am sure if they could do anything without endangering us, they would do so. We must wait.'

'*Wait!* How much longer? I think I will go mad with waiting. These people are churlish and sullen, Leowulf is a rude, barbaric animal and this place is a damp and draughty hovel——'

'Oh, Margo! If you can only whine and complain, please go away. If the Saxons are less than sympathetic towards you, you have only yourself to blame for you scarce endeared yourself to them at Erinwald. In over a year you have learned not a dozen words of their language, and treat them abominably. And as for Leowulf, I feel quite in sympathy with him, and all those like him. England is their country and we have taken it from them, and if it is ours by right of conquest, we can at least treat the people with a little civility. Can you blame them for wanting it back, or such small pieces of it as they can take back by any means? How would you feel if it were Normandy?'

'Adela!' Marguerite snapped the word in the tone of one rebuking an insolent child. And then did not seem to know how to continue. 'I do not understand you at all,' she said finally, and added sadly, 'You have changed a great deal since you came to England.'

'I would not have come had it not been forced upon me, and that you know! But I *am* here, and life would be far pleasanter if only we could live in peace with these people and try to give them cause to lose some of their hatred of us.'

Marguerite stared at her for a long moment, and then stood up. 'I think you should get some rest. You are not at all yourself, and I cannot think that you would say these things if you were.' She paused, and added more kindly, 'I know how you must feel about all this—but the Saxon is a fool, and Edward will never agree to a marriage. Try to sleep.'

When she had gone, Adela lay back on the bed and could not regret her outburst. They were things she had wanted to say to her these past six weeks, and had usually bitten her tongue instead. She felt a little better for having released some of the tension within her, but still had no answers for all those questions she kept asking herself about Leowulf.

Eventually she ceased to struggle with it all, and with a determined lift to her chin, she left the chamber and went into the hall. Children and dogs scrapped together in the rushes and

spilled outside, ignoring all the admonishings
of the women attending to their various tasks,
one or two of whom looked up and smiled as
Adela passed. Marguerite was again at the
tapestry, but she did not feel in any humour to
join her and went instead to the kitchen area in
search of some occupation to help pass the
time.

Frida and Edwina were there, and after a
little cajoling were reluctantly persuaded to
allow her to help them. Surprisingly, she spent
a very pleasant hour or so in the somewhat
crude surroundings, preparing what little food
there was to be eked out between the swollen
numbers of Leowulf's household. There would
be meagre fare if his hunting excursion was less
than successful.

As the day passed and Adela amused herself
with the children and working on the tapestry,
she was aware of a deference and a respect in
the manner of the Saxons towards her, that was
more genuine than anything they had shown
her at Erinwald. She puzzled over it for a while,
until it occurred to her that it was because of
Ewen. She, a Norman lady of noble birth, had
saved the life of a Saxon child at great risk to
herself, and that simple, instinctive action had
done more to earn her the respect and sympathy of the Saxons than all her endeavours
over the past months at Erinwald. Even the
men had lost some of their indifference.

There was a pleasant atmosphere in the hall,

and Adela felt almost at ease for the first time since Leowulf brought them there, which she could only attribute to the fact that he was away and she was able to relax.

'My lady——' Frida looked up from the tapestry and said shyly, 'My lady, I am sorry now that I betrayed your trust in me and did not warn you of Leowulf's coming.'

Adela, surprised, smiled. ''Tis forgiven, Frida. How could you have defied him? And you did try to aid our escape. We will not forget that.'

The Saxon girl ducked her head and murmured, 'Some of us have thought 'tis a pity you must hate him so, for we would not be displeased for him to have his way. There is none we would rather have as lady of Erinwald.'

Adela could do nothing but gaze at her for a moment or two, for there was suddenly an inexplicable lump in her throat. However, she was spared the need to answer by a sudden commotion outside. The door was thrown open and the tranquillity of the afternoon shattered, as Leowulf and his men spilled inside in noisy disarray.

No one did more than glance at the small deer that was flung upon the table. Leowulf himself, holding his cloak around him, strode tight-lipped across the hall and disappeared behind the curtains. The others threw themselves down on the benches or stood about with scowling faces. Several were wounded and

Frida limped away for her box of simples and dressings.

There was little Adela could do, and as the only words she could catch from the curses and angry mutterings of the men involved Normans and a 'cowardly attack', she withdrew from the confusion and stood to one side with Marguerite.

A few moments later, Frida called to her, and holding out a handful of her preparations, said quickly, 'They say my lord is hurt.'

Almost without thinking, Adela took the pots and linen and went at once to his chamber. He was seated in the chair with his back to her, his head bent to examine his shoulder; but as she entered, he started almost guiltily, pulled the cloak around him and turned to see who it was. The frown creasing his brow deepened. 'What is it?'

Undeterred by his tone, she came forward quietly and stood before him. 'You are hurt,' she said casually, 'and Frida is too busy attending to your men.'

' 'Tis nothing for you to concern yourself with,' he muttered, and turned away, dismissing her.

But the Lady Adela de Lise was not so easily dismissed. The signs of pain she detected on his face lent her courage and she bent down beside him. 'Come, my lord. Let me attend to it.'

'I'm not a child, wench,' he snapped. 'Do not talk to me as such.'

'Then you will let me treat your wound without making a fuss, will you not?' she replied sweetly, and was strangely reassured by the glare she received in reply.

He did, however, shift ever so slightly in the chair, and released his grip on the mantle. She freed the clasp and allowed it to fall away, drawing her fine brows together at the sight of the blood dried and matted on his tunic.

'You must lend me your knife, I think,' she said softly, holding out her hand. He made no move to give it to her and she raised her eyes to his with a query. 'Your knife?'

His eyes searched hers and she immediately understood. 'Do you think I would use it on *you*, my lord?' she asked him with a shadow of a smile. 'So little do you trust me. What have I to gain by such an action? Certainly not my freedom, for I have no doubt that I would get no further than the woods before your men caught me ... I have more respect than that for my life, and indeed more hopes for my survival without the need to resort to such measures.'

His eyes held hers, searching for some sign of trickery, and then, without taking his eyes from her face, took his knife from his belt and handed it to her.

She took it, conscious of somehow having gained something, and began, carefully, to cut away his tunic. But the blood had dried and made the fabric adhere to the wound, and she had to warm some water over the fire and soak it before lifting it gently away. Only the tautening of the muscles in his arm betrayed the pain he felt as she worked, and when he gave an almost inaudible sigh as the tunic came away and the ugly wound was exposed, she was strangely overcome by a strong desire to pull his head down upon her shoulder and comfort him for all the strength he must show simply because he was a man.

But she recovered quickly and ventured to ask what had happened. 'You were attacked, 'tis obvious, but——'

'By some of your countrymen, wench,' he replied sourly. 'Over-zealous boys who cannot tell a hunting party from a band of warriors.'

'Your men were not happy,' she said quietly. 'Perhaps they will not now be so content to follow you to William's side. Perhaps,' she added, 'you should abandon this quest.'

He regarded her quizzically. 'Do you never give up? Nay, I shall not abandon it.' He said no more but continued to watch her as she bathed the wound, dressed it and bound it with all the quick efficiency of one well used to such things. She was aware that he observed her, yet contrived not to blush under his gaze.

When she finished, she went back to the coffer at the foot of the bed and pulled out a tunic, which she held up for his approval. He nodded and she went forward to help him off with the one he wore, half-expecting to be pushed aside. But he made no demur, and indeed seemed grateful for her aid. It was not an easy task, for the wound greatly restricted the movement in his arm, but eventually it was done and the fresh tunic put on.

He donned his belt, took up the knife and went across to the door where he paused and looked back at her. 'My thanks, wench. You have a light touch.'

When he had gone, she stood for a moment staring at the closed door, with a slow warmth seeping through her at his grudging thanks, until suddenly she caught herself up on it and impatiently dismissed it as girlish embarrassment.

She shook herself and went to see whether Frida needed help, but she seemed to have successfully dealt with the casualties. Edith was hovering nearby, and Adela felt the hostility of her gaze like a cold draught across the width of the room. Had it been some of the men from whom this increased animosity came, she could, perhaps have accepted it more easily, for they had been needlessly attacked by her kind. But they all continued to treat her with civility, although persisting in showing complete indifference towards Marguerite.

She seemed, that evening, to find Edith and her coldness weighing very oppressively on her thoughts, and could not dismiss her from them even when she and Marguerite retired for the night. She lay staring up into the darkness, and could not sleep, going over in her mind everything that had happened to her during the past few days and desperately trying to make some sense out of her feelings about it all. She tossed and turned until she was totally exhausted by it all. And then out of the fog that seemed slowly to be closing in on her, came the clear, sensible, rational thought that tomorrow everything would be resolved, and she would be free of the Saxon and his problems and his arrogance and the power he seemed to be able to exercise over her. Tomorrow her uncle would come to take her back to Erinwald, and then, no doubt, Guy would take her back to Normandy.

Oh, for Normandy, she thought as sleep drifted in on her; Normandy before the invasion of England, when there had been peace and comfort and tranquillity, where nothing so violent or complicated or unpleasant had ever disrupted her life into the emotional turmoil that seemed to have beset her since the death of her father.

Tomorrow. If only tomorrow would hasten. If only all these vague, uncertain, half-formed fears she had about the outcome of it all were proven quite unfounded....

CHAPTER
SEVEN

FOOTSTEPS and hushed, whispering voices filled Adela's dreams that night with vague threats, and faces peered at her through the darkness, leering and mocking. And when she woke to discover that there had been some commotion during the night, cold tremors went through her at the thought that perhaps they had not been dreams after all.

Frida hastened her out of the chamber when she had dressed, for Leowulf wished to have some privacy to speak with his visitor. Adela began by hoping that it was a courier from her uncle, but Frida's slightly nervous manner dispelled that rather faint hope. It took her some while to discover the man's identity, for none seemed over-keen to impart the information to her, but eventually she overheard some snippet of conversation between a somewhat out of temper Edith and one of the older women, and her disappointment that there was no word from her uncle was quickly forgotten in a rush of indignation—Leowulf's visitor was a priest. And Leowulf spent most of the morning closeted with him.

'The audacity of this Saxon is beyond

everything!' she exclaimed in an angry whisper to Marguerite. 'He is so certain his will cannot be thwarted that he has a priest here to wed us already! 'Twould not surprise me had he sent for him before he even captured us!'

Yet beneath her anger and disgust, Adela was conscious of a tremor of apprehension which Marguerite's trite words of sympathy and reassurance, repeated often over the past two days, did nothing to dispel. She looked about for some other means to divert her thoughts and her gaze settled upon Olwyn, who was seated by the fire rather aimlessly whittling away at some wood.

She left Marguerite and went to sit on one of the stools close by him, pretending to be engrossed in examining the now faint red weals on her wrists. After a moment or two, she turned casually towards him and asked what he was carving.

He looked up and almost smiled. ''Tis nothing. Perhaps a toy for a pretty wench.'

She began to make a polite comment, but her attention was diverted by the sight of Leowulf emerging from behind the curtain with the priest and her words trailed off as she watched them disappear into the kitchen. Then, moments later, Leowulf returned alone and went towards the door, but Edith disengaged herself from her conversation and hastened to detain him. Their discussion seemed serious and although Adela could not see Edith's face, she could clearly see her gestures and the earnestness of them suggested that she was pleading with him. Did she think a man such as he could be diverted from his course by the pleas of a love-sick maid?

' 'Tis no great wonder she dislikes me so,' she murmured. 'To love such a man and have him bring a priest to wed him to another for the most mercenary of reasons is surely a sickening thing.'

'You believe the wench ... *loves* Leowulf?' Olwyn said in a strange tone.

Adela turned to him, wide-eyed. 'Is it not obvious? Her eyes are full of love whenever she is near him, and 'tis there for all to see.' She turned her head to observe the couple, Leowulf—tall, strong, imperious, showing no sign that he had been wounded; Edith—small, slender, pretty with her blue eyes now full of appeal. Leowulf put his hand on the girl's shoulder and shook her gently. It was an intimate gesture and Adela averted her gaze. 'See how obvious it is?' she said quietly and raised her eyes to Olwyn's face. 'You are close to him. Has he not said anything of his feelings for her? Perhaps,' she added casually, 'she will be lady of this place, for 'tis certain he will not have his way in this other matter. She has no cause to worry so.'

Olwyn, however, made no reply. There was an odd expression on his face and his eyes were

staring fixedly at the couple. When they went
to the door and went outside, he put down
his wood and his knife and followed them, and
she was left gazing after him, bewildered and
wondering.

She sat alone for a few minutes until
Marguerite came to join her, but they had little
to say to each other. It was the fervent hope in
both their minds that Edward would hasten
back from the King and bring a swift end to
their confinement with Leowulf, but as they
seemed only to become out of temper when
they discussed the situation and there was little
they could do but wait, they both remained
silent with their own thoughts. That Marguerite could not decide whether she was more
angry with Leowulf than she was bored, was
obvious, but Adela had many things on her
mind which she could not confide to Marguerite, and she was content to sit quietly and pon-
der over them.

She was shaken out of her daydreams, however, by the return of Olwyn. Edith was hanging on his arm as they came back into the hall
and she was looking up into his face with that
same shining look in her eyes. They were talking softly and as Olwyn laughed at something
she said, Edith squeezed herself closer against
him and rested her head against his arm. He
put his hand up to the long golden hair falling
down her back and bent his head to kiss her
forehead.

Adela drew a sharp breath. Was it *Olwyn*, then, whom the Saxon girl loved? She stared at them, trying to recall if Olwyn had always been with Leowulf when she had seen Edith look towards him in that way.

She turned away so that her back was towards them, her eyes wide with sudden speculation. 'My lady?' Adela turned her head to find Frida standing before her. 'Is anything amiss? You look so strange——'

'Nay, Frida,' she said, with a slight shake of her head. 'There is nothing amiss. But I am curious.' She paused, and knowing that Marguerite would not understand the conversation, went on: 'Who is Edith? She did not leave Erinwald with Leowulf when my uncle came, that I know. But she has such hostility in her that I cannot help but be curious.'

Frida seemed to hesitate for a moment or two, as if undecided whether to share what she knew. She pushed one of the dogs away with her foot and eventually said: 'I know only what I have heard from others. Her family was killed by the Normans when William's army marched to London after the great battle. She fled, and lived over at Wycke until the Normans came there too. She arrived here near starving soon after my lord came here, and he said she could stay as long as she wished.'

'I have seen them together,' Adela said carefully. 'They seem ... close. She is more than fond of him?'

Frida shook her head. 'I think they are close, but 'tis only natural. He feels responsible for her, I think, for she has no family and he has offered her his protection and she is grateful. But 'tis Olwyn she loves, and he will have none of her. Or would not,' she amended quickly, glancing towards them as they disappeared through the curtain. 'I think perhaps 'tis happily resolved now.'

Adela nodded and Frida limped away, having quite forgotten what it was she had come to ask.

'What were you talking about?' Marguerite asked, resentment tinging her voice.

'Nothing, Margo. Nothing of importance.' Marguerite said something more, but Adela was not listening; she wished merely to be left alone to think and to make some sense of the chaos into which her thoughts had been plunged once more.

Edith loved *Olwyn*, not Leowulf. So it was probable that her hostility was not merely jealousy, but it was because Adela was a Norman and she did not want Leowulf to wed a Norman nor to have anyone with Norman blood as the lady of Erinwald.

Why she should feel so relieved, she was not sure, but she had little time to trouble over it, for Leowulf strode in calling for food and ale, and behind him came two men. Adela's heart jolted and left her a little breathless, for she recognised the second of them as one of her uncle's retainers. The other was doubtless the Saxon who had been waiting for him. 'Marguerite! 'Tis Alain Harfleur!'

But Marguerite had already seen them and was rising to her feet with such an expression of relief and excitement on her face that Adela's own sudden rush of hope turned into alarm and she reached out and caught her aunt's arm, pulling her back.

'Margo, don't be foolish!' she whispered harshly. 'Wait a while. We must not anger Leowulf now or he may never let us go.'

It was easy for her to say such things to her aunt, but as Marguerite sank back on to the stool Adela found her foot tapping the floor in impatience and her whole body tense with nerves.

Leowulf's deep voice resounded through the crude wooden building. 'Come, my Saxons. This man is from Sir Edward de Lise and William of Normandy. What he has to say will affect not myself alone but all of you. Come close and hear his words.' His intense blue gaze rested on Adela and he beckoned.

In some trepidation Adela rose, conscious of Marguerite beside her, and walked with her, with as much dignity as she could muster, to stand before him. What would she do if he refused to admit he was defeated and would not release them? And what would happen to him and his Saxons? She was feeling sorry for the Saxon Lion despite herself. He should have

found some other way to achieve peace with
William.

Alain Harfleur took a step forward, hesitated, then took Marguerite's hand, bowed
over it and said, 'My lady. You are well?'

'As well as can be expected, Alain. What
news?'

Harfleur, however, turned to Adela, took
her hand also and bowed over it. 'And you, my
lady?'

'Yes, Alain, thank you, I am well. We have
been …' she glanced fleetingly at the Saxon,
'… reasonably treated. Is my—is Sir Edward
close by? What is to happen now? Are
we——?' She broke off at the expression on
Harfleur's face and was suddenly filled with
dread.

The man was nervous; his eyes kept flicker-
ing from her to Leowulf and back again. But
Leowulf was far from nervous and looked at
her with his steady blue eyes. 'It seems, little
one,' he said in French, 'that the King agrees to
my terms. All my terms.'

Adela was quite still for several moments
and remained calm as she turned to Harfleur
for confirmation.

'My lady, 'tis true. Sir Edward has sent me to
relay the King's terms.'

'And they are?' Her voice shook very
slightly.

'The King will meet with Leowulf at Erinwald tomorrow. If he is in good faith, William

will accept him as a subject and restore Erinwald in return for his loyalty and his aid in bringing to him in peace other Saxons still in hiding in the hills. As a measure of *his* goodwill, the King also agrees to a marriage between you, my lady, and the Saxon Leowulf, and he will attend the ceremony himself at Erinwald. It is also a term of his agreement to this, that you have four of Sir Edward's best men to attend you and protect you during the first year of such a marriage.'

There was a faint murmur amongst the Saxons, as those who had understood this whispered it to those who had not.

Adela stood perfectly still; nothing seemed real. She stared at the man before her, unaware of his discomfort, and in a voice totally unlike her own, she said: 'And what had my uncle to say? Is there some word from him for me?'

There was something in the way he looked at her, as if he were trying to tell her something. 'My lady, Sir Edward said only that the King's wish is *his* wish; you should do his bidding and trust him.' There was an intensity about his words as he said this, but as she met his gaze she could not clearly understand what he was trying to say to her. Her mind was too cloudy and her thoughts too scattered for her to interpret whether it was warning or reassurance.

She shifted her gaze to the Saxon. He was looking at her, but without the self-satisfied triumphant gleam in his eyes she had expected to see. His expression was quite serious and he returned her look of bewilderment and confusion steadily. 'This cannot be true,' she whispered, turning to her aunt. 'Margo——' Marguerite, however, had no comforting words now, and her expression was as confused and bewildered as Adela's own.

She made a desperate attempt to steady herself, but her thoughts were wild. How was it possible that William, a man said by all those who knew him to be a just and a fair man, could calmly give his blessing to the marriage of a lady of Normandy to a Saxon barbarian with a reputation that could scarcely be described as endearing? But William put the well-being of many before the happiness and safety of one—and what was the sacrifice of one young maid against the possible loyalty of many erstwhile enemies? Their loyalty or their capture—whichever it was, a ruler such as William would not hesitate to risk one young maid for such rewards.

Contrarily, these thoughts seemed to bring Adela a kind of cold composure. She looked up at Leowulf and in his language, so that all could hear and understand, she said icily, 'You cannot force me to wed you, Saxon.'

'I will not force you,' he said quietly. 'But I think you will not dare disobey your King's wishes.'

The King's wishes. The thought was chilling, and she had no answer. Quite suddenly she could not stand there any longer with all eyes upon her, so with her head held high, pride and dignity in every line of her body, she turned away and as she began to walk towards the bedchambers, the Saxons drew aside to let her pass unhindered.

CHAPTER
EIGHT

MARGUERITE followed Adela into the bed-chamber and made vain attempts to reassure her. She was convinced that it was merely a trick to lure Leowulf down to Erinwald where it would be easier to capture him. Indeed, Adela tried desperately to convince herself that this was so, for she could not bear to believe that her uncle, and Guy, would allow her to be used by the King for such petty political gains.

And yet, would they be able to defy him? She did not know what to think or believe, and the mere fact that thinking of Leowulf tricked and captured in such a way could cause her to feel so disturbed, confused her even further, and she paced up and down the room, agitated and angry.

'We must escape, Margo,' she said rather desperately. ''Tis the only way. For what will happen to me if——' She broke off as the door opened, and Frida came in with a summons for Marguerite to go to Leowulf, and a drinking horn of mulled ale. When Marguerite had gone, with disparaging words about him but a hopeful look in her eyes, Frida proffered the over-full horn. 'My lord gave me this for you, my lady,' she said. 'He thought you may be in need of it.'

'That was very generous of him,' she said, her voice hard with a mixture of bitterness and sarcasm. 'But 'tis something more than ale I need to soothe my temper.' Nevertheless, she accepted it and sat down in the chair by the fire, and although she would have admitted it to no one, she was grateful for it, for the news had left her cold, and the warm, fragrant ale was soothing.

'My lady,' the Saxon girl began timidly, 'if it happens that you must wed Leowulf, there is not one of us who will not try to help you and make it easier for you. We would all like to have you as Leowulf's lady.'

Adela smiled a little. 'Yes, Frida, I know, and it helps a great deal.'

When the girl had gone, she drank her ale and as a little of the initial panic subsided, she stared into the flames lost in thought. She had no idea how long she sat there. The room, already gloomy with the shutters excluding most of the light, grew quite dark, and she did not bother to light the torch. She tried to think what life would be like if she had no choice but to marry Leowulf; but the prospect aroused only fear in her and she thought longingly of Normandy before all this. Escape seemed impossible. If, indeed, it was the King's will, and her uncle could do nothing against him, where could she go? For her own sake, she could only hope Marguerite was right and Leowulf was captured at Erinwald. Yet she could not, somehow, bring herself to hate him enough to wish for that.

'Adela.' The deep, gentle voice and the light from the torch he had put in the wall-sconce roused her and she looked round at Leowulf as he seated himself on the coffer at the foot of the bed.

As she looked at him, his hand moved unconsciously to his shoulder and began slowly to rub it as if to relieve the pain. His brows were drawn together and there were lines of strain on his face, where the marks made by Marguerite's nails seemed livid against its pallor.

'The wound pains you?' she asked, trying to sound as though she did not care whether it did or not.

'Yea, wench, it hurts like hell's thorns, though none save you and I shall know it.' She merely looked at him and made no comment. 'But 'tis not the wound that troubles me,' he went on in more serious vein, 'but your accursed uncle.' Again she said nothing, but continued to return his gaze steadily. 'I fear 'tis necessary we be wed tonight.'

'Tonight?' she echoed incredulously. 'You are mad!'

'Not mad, wench, merely mindful. There is some falseness here.'

She shook her head. 'My uncle would not

give his word falsely. Nor would the King.'

'You know little of men, wench,' he replied in an almost indulgent tone. 'Your uncle's man had not the look of one who has travelled from London in such weather. And how long do you suppose it would take a man to ride such a distance in the snow?'

'Perhaps the King was not in London, and he had not to go so far.'

The Saxon nodded. 'Perhaps, but I cannot take any risk now of losing——' He stopped abruptly and went on, 'Of losing Erinwald. So we must be wed tonight.'

She shook her head. 'No. 'Tis impossible. I will not agree to such a thing. If it must be, then it will be at Erinwald tomorrow when I can satisfy myself 'tis truly the wish of my uncle and the King.'

He was silent for a moment as he stretched out his long legs. 'There are several things you should consider,' he began slowly. 'Your uncle would have you trust him and do his bidding, is that not what Harfleur said? And if you truly believe your uncle and the King would not give their word falsely, then you must believe 'tis their wish we be wed. The King's wish. And you dare not refuse that.'

He glanced at her, but she looked away into the flames of the fire, and he continued: 'But I believe they are playing me false. So you and I will be wed tonight and tomorrow return to Erinwald. The Lady Marguerite and Harfleur will remain here, and if all is well, they will be released in good time. If there is some trick....' He left the suggestion unfinished.

'You would not dare harm them!' she challenged, turning her head abruptly to look at him.

'There is very little I would not dare, wench, and you should know that. I hope such measures will not be necessary.'

'But if you use them as hostages, why do you demand we be wed tonight? There is no point to it. Do you jest? Do you torment me deliberately simply to amuse yourself?'

He laughed. 'Nay, wench. But when we go to Erinwald I would have the thing done, and you will convince them that you are well pleased with it.' He held up his hand to prevent her interruption. 'And it seems my Saxons have taken you to their hearts, and I cannot now have them turn against me. So I need your aid. I need them to see that I go to William with a Norman wife—one who has wed me willingly and believes in the joining of our two peoples.'

'You expect too much,' she stated flatly and looked away into the fire.

He did not answer immediately, and when she looked around again to discover the reason for his silence, he said in a softer tone, 'Do not despair, little one. If I am captured, you will be free and have suffered no ill, and doubtless William will declare the marriage annulled. If

all is well, you will be wed to the lord of Erinwald under William's protection and I will do
you no harm. Indeed, if you then still wish to
leave and return to your uncle or to Normandy,
I will not prevent you.'

'Oh! How generous you are! But what use is
that to me? Guy would have none of me, and
'tis Guy I love.'

'Nay, Adela.' His voice was gentle and after
a moment he rose and came to bend down
before her. 'Guy de Brec is betrothed. He is
betrothed to a lady of the court with some claim
to kinship with William.'

She stared at him for a moment, and then
shook her head, smiling a little. 'Such lies will
not make me do your bidding, Saxon!'

'I know how it must hurt you, little one,' he
said gently. 'Women have strange notions over
such things, but 'tis the truth. I have it from
Harfleur, and what cause would he have to
lie?'

Adela began to feel a little sick, and leaned
back in the chair closing her eyes. 'Go away,
Saxon. This ale and your presence have made
me sick and I would like a little peace. Why do
you torment me?'

He rose and straightened, and stood looking
down at her. 'I will leave you for a little while,
but I will return for your answer. Think carefully on all that I have said. I am sorry it is this
way, but there is no helping it now. In other
circumstances....' He stopped and shrugged,

'But then, 'tis done now and we must see how it all comes about.'

He left her then, and as the door closed behind him, it was as if a cold draught came into the room in his place and she shivered, and bent forward to put another log on the fire. His strength and the power he seemed able to exert over her alternately angered and frightened her, and she sat there completely at a loss to know what to do.

It should not, she knew, be a very difficult thing to merely refuse to do his bidding. No one could force her to marry him. And yet, if it was the King's wish, if all he said were true and if he should do as he had threatened, what choice had she? What else was there for her to do? She already knew that escape was impossible. She did not for a moment believe that Guy was betrothed, but she could not understand why he would allow this to happen to her....

In the hour she was left alone, she tried to think of every possible way of extricating herself from this problem, but eventually she gave up. There was no way out that did not further endanger Marguerite. Her head throbbed; she felt sick. She could take no more. She leaned back in the chair with her eyes closed and knew she would give in.

With this knowledge, however, there also came a strength and a resolution. She was a well-born lady of Normandy and she would be treated as such. If he believed he would be wed to a meek, yielding young girl who would do his bidding at a mere word and come to heel at his whistle, he would find himself in a sorry state, for she would be no such thing.

When he returned for her answer, she was outwardly very calm and no sign showed on her face of the turmoil and helplessness within her, but she found it difficult to look at him fully when she spoke.

'I—I believe I have little choice, my lord. I will wed you tonight because I fear for the safety of Marguerite, and I will do so with as much grace as possible, for it is inconceivable that the Lady Adela de Lise could act otherwise. But you must know 'tis not my wish, and I agree to it only because I see no other course open to me.'

Leowulf inclined his head almost regally, acknowledging her acceptance of the situation as if he had expected nothing less. 'Such a pretty, proud speech does you credit, my lady,' he said, putting a little more emphasis on the 'my lady' than was warranted. 'Well, so be it. I will send Frida to help you prepare yourself.'

Frida came in with the one gown which had been brought from Erinwald for her which she had not worn, and it was with the strangest sensations fluttering in her stomach that she prepared for her wedding.

She was making the final adjustments to the gold-threaded girdle about her hips when the door opened and Leowulf walked in with seemingly no concern at all for the state of undress in which she might have been. She glared at him, which had not the slightest effect upon him, and turned her back on him while she and Frida attended to the final details of her dress and she began to comb her hair. He had made some effort in his own attire, and despite the tumult going on within her, she was aware that he looked as fine as he had done when they had gone to meet her uncle a few days ago, although he had tactfully omitted the weapons from his trappings.

He stood watching her silently, with a gleam of amusement in his eyes at her evident discomfort, and as she grew more and more angry at the way he seemed to her to be enjoying the unfortunate position he had forced upon her, her face suffused with colour. Eventually she turned round and said crossly, 'I trust you are enjoying this, my lord, for I assure you I am not, and I almost hope it is a trick and you are taken prisoner at Erinwald tomorrow.'

Leowulf merely smiled broadly. 'Yea, but 'tis that "almost" which betrays you, little one. I am well content that this will all come out right in time.'

She coloured darkly and turned abruptly away, tugging the comb viciously through her long hair; then, tossing the comb aside, she pulled one half of the silky mass over her shoulder and began to braid it with swift and practised ease.

'Nay, leave it,' he interrupted her. ''Tis better so.'

She looked at him with hostility flashing in her eyes, but after a moment she shrugged her shoulders and let her hair fall, tossing her head so that it fell down her back, and she stood with passive disinterest as Frida combed it again.

When she was ready, and he was seemingly satisfied with what he saw as he let his gaze slide over her slender form, he took her firmly by the arm and led her from the chamber. In the passageway outside, she pulled back and looked up at him. 'What of Marguerite? You promised....'

His eyes glinted with a sudden gleam of amusement. 'The lady Marguerite left for Erinwald with Harfleur nearly two hours since.'

Adela drew a sharp breath and her eyes flashed the anger that surged through her veins. 'You have tricked me,' she whispered in a voice trembling with suppressed fury. 'You are—you are the most hateful, loathsome....'

He chuckled and patted her arm. 'Nay, nay. It makes no difference. That was but a small thing in the terms of this arrangement.'

She averted her gaze and chewed her lip, unable to answer. 'You are over-fond of *terms*, my lord.'

''Tis something your William has brought

to England,' he answered. 'Devious talk and trickery and treaties, to replace our Saxon strength and force of arms.'

'You have lost nothing of your force, Saxon.'

He merely smiled and took her arm again. 'Come. The priest is waiting.'

CHAPTER
NINE

THE hall was only dimly lit, for several of the torches were missing from the sconces; the priest stood at the far end with the Saxons forming a wide arc on either side of him. Feeling as though at any moment she would either be sick, or faint, Adela paused with Leowulf for a moment as he surveyed the scene with some satisfaction. She felt the departure of Marguerite acutely, although she could not wish her back, and she felt herself suddenly very alone. She thought fleetingly of the journey from Erinwald only a few days ago; how she had clenched her fists and gritted her teeth so that he would not know how the ropes round her wrists were hurting her; and how determined she had been to prove that Norman ladies were made of a tougher fibre. But the cause of it seemed paltry beside the troubles that beset her now—and what use was her Norman pride?

They went forward slowly until they stood before the priest, and although she had been unable to think clearly of anything, many things went through her thoughts in those few moments. What would happen if she broke free

of Leowulf's grip on her arm and shouted out
that she hated him, that Marguerite was safe
and she could not, and would not be forced to
wed him? Would any of these Saxons risk
Leowulf's anger and vengeance to help her?
And Guy? Could there possibly be some truth
in Leowulf's story that he was betrothed?

The priest began to speak. Did he know why
he had been asked to marry a Saxon rebel and a
Norman lady in this forsaken hut in the hills in
the middle of the night?

It was the King's wish that this should be.
Adela raised her head and pulled back her
shoulders. She must remember that. Alain
Harfleur had brought the King's message—if
Leowulf was in good faith, he would accept him
as a subject, restore him to Erinwald and agree
to a marriage between them. And one thing she
could not doubt was that Leowulf wanted
peace now between Saxon and Norman. So she
would have had to marry him at the King's wish
anyway, which was, to any subject, no different
from a command. What difference was there in
wedding him at Erinwald tomorrow, or
tonight, here?

The Lady Adela de Lise was married to
Leowulf, Lord of Erinwald with none of the
splendour and ceremony which usually sur-
rounded the wedding of a member of the de
Lise family. And if she had none of the shyness
or sparkling eyes of a young maiden on her
wedding day, there was none there who noticed

it or remarked upon it.

When it was over, she felt numb, and a silent, grave-faced Leowulf took her arm and led her back towards the bedchambers amidst the smiles and quiet congratulations of the Saxons, which Adela barely noticed and yet responded to without realising that she did so. The Saxons would have followed them into the chamber, to see them bedded in riotous fashion as was the usual custom; but Leowulf bade them stay and drink to his health and that of his bride. And with a torch someone thrust into his hand, he drew Adela away, and led her through the curtained doorway to the darkness beyond.

They stood alone in the bedchamber, and Adela recovered some of her usual spirit and forced a smile. 'So, my lord, we are wed,' she said in a voice that trembled a little, and looking at him for the first time. 'I trust you are satisfied?'

The expression on his face, however, was not one of satisfaction. He nodded slightly and said, 'I will be more so if all comes out as it should tomorrow.' He looked at her for a long moment, took a step forward and then checked, seeming to change his mind. He sighed, rubbed at his shoulder and half-turned away. 'You are tired, wench. Go to bed and sleep, for tomorrow we must arise early.' He turned on his heel and left the room, closing the door behind him and leaving her alone.

He did not, then, expect her to be a wife to him tonight. With relief she turned towards the bed and began to undress and when she had quenched the torch and crept beneath the pelts, she lay for a long time listening to the sounds of revelry from the hall, wondering if he were with them or whether he took his pleasure of some other wench.

The relief ebbed slowly away and left an emptiness in the pit of her stomach and a painful lump rose into her throat and tears stung her eyes. She had known, had she not, that he took her as his wife merely for politics? So what else did she expect of him? Why did she lie there listening for the sound of the door opening? Why did she feel so wretched because it remained so firmly closed? *Why?*

Then, quite suddenly, she ceased to struggle with her emotions and admitted to herself what she had been denying all along. She was in love with the Saxon. She did not know quite when it had happened, but thought perhaps she had loved him, and denied it, since he had cut the ropes from her wrists. And now she was married to him. Far from causing her any feelings of warmth and happiness, however, it made her aware only of a seeping misery. For how could she bear to love him, and live with him as his wife, knowing that he had married her only to regain control of Erinwald and to protect it, himself and his people from the Norman King? How many nights would she have to lie alone in their bed as she did now, wondering where he was? Would it always be like this? Would she ever be able to make him love her?

Admitting that she was in love with him was, somehow, worse than the confusion and anger she had felt before. Adela turned her head away from the door, closing her eyes tightly on the tears that squeezed out between her lashes and clenched her fists until her nails dug into her palms....

Eventually she slept, and the tears dried on her face.

She awoke with a start some while later. There was no sound now from the hall and she lay listening intently for whatever noise had awoken her. After a moment or two there were three steady taps on the shutter at the window. With a thumping heart, she rose and wrapped her mantle around her shoulders and went over to it.

She stood on her toes with her face upturned and whispered, 'Who's there? What do you want?'

'Adela?'

Her heart gave a leap of excitement and she forgot to whisper. 'Guy! What are you——?'

'Be quiet, you fool! Are you all right?'

'Yes, of course.'

'Can you get out?'

'I—I don't know. Wait——' She ran to the

door and opened it just enough to peer outside. The tapestry curtain was only pulled halfway across the opening and the light from a torch still left burning in the hall enabled her to see that there was no one on guard in the passageway. She walked softly to the curtain, unconsciously holding her breath, and glanced swiftly around the hall. She could see no one awake, only many bodies lying hunched beneath furs and skins on pallets on the floor, and one or two slumped over their ale at the table. Leowulf was apparently very sure that marriage would rob her of a desire to flee from him!

On the way back to her room, she glanced briefly at the closed door of the adjoining bedchamber behind which, she supposed Leowulf lay sleeping, and she paused there, staring at that closed door.

Leowulf. She loved him, but for her own sake she could not live with him knowing that he had no such feelings for her. She had married him as the King wished, but there had been no mention of having to remain with him. She would plead her case with the King if necessary, but surely, now that Guy had come, they could flee; not to Normandy, but somewhere out of William's domain, and she could be happy with Guy. Leowulf did not really need her to accomplish his ambitions. If she fled in the night his Saxons could blame him for nothing, and they would all stay loyal to him, and William could not blame him for her disappearance....

She turned and went swiftly back to her room, abruptly closing her mind to any other doubts and arguments. She had to go with Guy.

'Guy?' She stood at the window and whispered breathlessly. 'I believe I could get as far as the door, but it will surely awaken someone when I open it.' There was silence for a moment and Adela began to panic. 'Guy?'

'Hush. You must risk it. You are small enough to need only a crack to slip through. Go now and hurry.'

Her heart was thumping violently, and her head buzzing with questions and doubts, but she dressed swiftly and with her mantle clasped around her shoulders, crept outside. Once through the curtain, she drew a slow, deep breath and held it, tense and alert for the slightest sound as she picked her way carefully through the sleeping shapes on the floor.

The dogs that had been sleeping in a pile by the glowing remains of the fire looked up, ears erect, and stared at her, but none of them did more than whimper. At the door, she let out her breath and drew another; then carefully, inch by inch, she lifted the heavy bar, wincing each time it scraped against the wood, and set it down against the wall. The door was heavy and she had to bite her lips together to prevent a gasp of exertion escaping her. It made only a

faint creak as she pulled it open barely enough
to enable her to squeeze herself through the
opening, out into the cold night air.

She stood very still, listening intently, and
started with a gasp as Guy's hand closed round
her arm.

'Guy! How glad I am to see you!' She could
see, by the dim light through the open door,
that he smiled.

'Come,' he said. 'We must hurry.'

She moved swiftly and quietly with him until
they stood beside his horse tethered in the
trees. 'Were there no guards?' she murmured.
'How did you know which was my room?'

He lifted her up so that she sat sideways
across the saddle and mounted behind her,
curling one arm around her waist. 'There were
two guards. One is dead—I could not help that.
The other lies unconscious and tied to a tree
yonder. Marguerite told me where you have
been kept and that the window had been
shuttered to prevent you trying to escape
again.'

They moved at a walking pace through the
trees and were silent until they emerged further
along the rough road down which she and
Marguerite had made their bid for escape. It
was dark; the thin sliver of moon high in the
star-kissed sky gave barely enough light to
enable them to travel at a canter in safety, but
Guy was concerned only with putting as great a
distance between them and the Saxons as poss-

ible, and the horses' hooves on the ground made the only sound in the eerily quiet night.

Adela rested her head against his chest, and as she did so she felt something metal hanging round his neck. She put a hand up to touch it; it seemed to be the shape of a flower or the sun, with a stone in its centre. 'What is this?' she enquired softly and added with a mischievous smile, 'Is it loot?'

'Adela! You should know better! Nay...' He paused for a long moment and then went on, 'I did bring it back, but 'tis a talisman, gold and ruby. A gift.'

'A gift? Who would give you such a gift?' She asked, merely from curiosity, but he was silent so long that she thought perhaps she had upset him. 'I did not mean——'

'Nay, 'tis right you should know. 'Tis a betrothal gift, Adela.'

It was Adela's turn to be silent. So it was true. She was not hurt. Indeed, she was surprised to find herself relieved. She would *not* have been happy with him, loving Leowulf as she did. She could admit that now.

'I am pleased for you,' she said softly, as they slowed to a walk to negotiate a steep slope in almost total darkness as the moon disappeared behind the trees.

'Truly?' he answered. 'I know what has been in your heart and mind these last months, Adela, and I would not like to hurt you. But Isabelle is—She is....' He seemed at a loss for words and finished: 'But you will meet her soon enough.'

'Meet her? But how——?' She broke off, remembering what Leowulf had told her. 'She is some kin to William, is she not? Will she—will you speak to him for me, then? Otherwise where am I to go? There is nowhere—no one. . . .'

'I do not understand,' he said, obviously puzzled. 'Have you been ... harmed? Did the Saxon—*hurt* you?'

'No, of course not,' she replied, equally puzzled. 'We have been surprisingly well treated. The things that are said of Leowulf seem to me to be a Saxon legend in the making!' Even as she spoke, she felt a strange churning in her stomach and a coldness begin to creep over her.

She felt him stiffen behind her. 'But Marguerite said—she was in quite a state. She collapsed when Harfleur brought her back, and complained of such coarse treatment and ill-usage——'

'Oh, but she exaggerates! You know how she is!'

'Yea, but it put your uncle in such a temper that he sent me to bring you out of there, and is even now on his way to destroy the Saxon and burn that place to the ground!'

Adela twisted round and stared at him in the darkness, filled with horror. 'What? Oh! Oh, no! But—but does the King know? Surely if he has agreed to meet Leowulf tomorrow, he would not—oh, but was it then a trap after all, and he meant to take him prisoner...?'

Panic rose in her and her heart thumped wildly as her thoughts raced ahead of her words and she grew incoherent.

'What are you talking about?' Guy interrupted. 'Adela, I know that Alain did not have the chance to speak with you alone, but he was to tell you if he could that we did not go to the King, and it was merely a ruse to lure the Saxon to Erinwald. Surely you did not believe we would wish you to—What the——!'

'Stop! Guy, stop this horse——!' She tugged hard on the reins, causing the poor creature to rear up, and she slipped from her precarious seat to the ground and stood out of the way until Guy had brought the startled animal back under control.

'What in God's name——?' he began angrily.

'Tell me the truth of it,' she demanded. 'My uncle has not been to the King at all? He has been waiting at Erinwald for three days while any sort of horror could have been happening to us? He has tried to trick Leowulf into walking into a trap and butcher him and God knows how many others? And now, because Marguerite has been telling all manner of lies about him, he is on his way to burn and murder....' Her voice faltered but she recovered quickly. 'What kind of men are you? You, who have called Leowulf animal! Take me back. We must go back and warn them!'

'What? You are mad!'

Adela, however, saw only a vision of the dream she had had that first night as Leowulf's prisoner; she had looked back over Guy's shoulder and seen Leowulf at the window with the flames all around him, consuming him. All sense of reason fled from her. She flew at Guy and tried desperately to pull him from the horse, thinking of nothing but a frantic need to go back. Tears of anger and frustration blinded her as her almost hysterical attempts to make Guy agree to take her back only succeeded in making him lose his temper with her. Eventually he leapt from the horse, grasped her arms in an iron grip and shook her nearly senseless.

'For God's sake, be still! You ungrateful little brat! What do you care what happens to a Saxon barbarian who would as soon kill you as look at you? Do you realise the danger you have been in? If you have not been harmed it is a blessed mercy and you can thank God for it——'

'And you and my uncle seemed to have cared nothing for that while you hid at Erinwald and slept easy in your beds!' she flung back at him.

'Be quiet and let's be gone from here before Edward and the others——'

'No!' She screamed the word at him and tried to pull away from him, but he did not loosen his grip on her and she suddenly stopped struggling and looked at him helplessly. 'Why? Why is my uncle doing this? Why did he not go to the King? He gave his *word*, Guy.'

'Adela, I love you like my sister, but at this moment I could easily——' He broke off and sighed, and glanced around in exasperation. 'Is it necessary to discuss this now? You may have all the explanations you need back at Erinwald.'

Adela stared at him for a moment unable, in the darkness to see his face properly, and then, with a little gasp of anger and misery, she whirled round and set off in the direction from which they had come, half-walking, half running, conscious only of Leowulf and the danger he was in, and her own desperate need to reach him before her uncle.

Guy turned his horse with a curse and came after her, reining in ahead of her and blocking the path. 'Don't you understand?' he demanded. 'When your uncle came to claim Erinwald in William's name, he allowed the Saxon to escape; he should have brought him to his knees then and made him vow allegiance to our King. 'Tis his fault the Saxon "lion",' he said the word with a sneer and she winced, 'has roamed the hills these past three months, taking vengeance on our patrols and hunting parties. If Edward had gone to the King and told him that his wife and niece were abducted and such impossible terms demanded, the King's anger would have come down upon him, your uncle, for not dealing with this Saxon troublemaker before, and not upon the Saxon himself. Edward had to deal with this himself——'

'Stop!' she cried. 'I will hear no more! Take me back to warn him, or be gone back to Erinwald and allow *me* to go on alone. My uncle is a fool, and if Leowulf is killed this night there will be such a rising of Saxons that the King will curse the very name of de Lise!' She made a movement to go around him, but his horse reared up and she shrank back. 'Guy, please——' she whispered, a catch in her voice.

'Why?' he demanded. 'Why do you care so much what happens to this Saxon cur? Do you realise that if Edward had gone to William you would very likely have *had* to marry him?'

She stood very still. In the silence, a wolf howled in the distance, an eerie sound that echoed through the night, and Guy's horse snorted nervously and pawed at the ground. 'Guy,' she began slowly, 'I *am* married to him. We were wed by a priest tonight. I was threatened and had no choice, but——' She raised her head defiantly. 'But I am glad of it now, and proud. Rather would I be the wife of such a man, Saxon rebel or not, than be wed to the like of you and my uncle, who would murder innocent women and children for the unproven crimes of a man trying only to win back freedom for himself and his people in the country we have stolen from them. I love him, Guy, and you will not stop me going back to him. I should not have come with you.'

She turned quickly, plunged into the trees and began to run. It was too dark for her to see anything and all she had to guide her were the vicious lash of low branches and spiky bushes, and the darker shadows that were tree-trunks.

But Guy was only a moment behind her, and quickly caught her. As his hand closed on her arm and pulled her up short, wrenching her round, a blind red rage seemed to sweep over her and in near-hysteria she flew at him, punching, screaming, scratching and struggling until, in near-exhaustion, she collapsed against his chest, sobbing and pleading with him. 'He must not be killed, Guy, please. Please. Take him to William as a prisoner if you must, and I will plead for him, but....'

He was silent for what seemed to her an hour, and then he sighed, pushing her away and holding her at arm's length. 'Come, then. We will go back.'

She looked up at him; hope flowed through her like a warm liquid and she gave him a swift, grateful hug, and began to make her way back through the trees to his horse.

CHAPTER
TEN

SHE had not realised they had come so far, and
going back seemed to take an eternity. They
went in silence, Guy because he had to concentrate now on moving even more quickly without setting the horse in a rut and laming him,
and Adela because her every nerve was tense,
silently urging Guy to hurry and fretting at
every slowing of their pace.

Eventually they rounded a clump of trees
and emerged into the large clearing, at the far
side of which were the stark shadows of
Leowulf's makeshift homestead and its litter of
untidy outbuildings. Adela sprang from the
horse before Guy had even pulled him up; she
stumbled as she touched the ground, recovered, lifted the skirt of her gown above her
knees and ran recklessly over the uneven
ground. Her escape had evidently been discovered, for there was more light behind the
skins across the windows and the door she had
left slightly ajar was closed.

In her haste to reach Leowulf, she threw
herself against the door, stumbled as it flew
open and fell across the threshold in a crumpled heap. There was a stunned silence. Adela

looked up and met the steely blue gaze of
Leowulf glaring at her across the width of the
hall. He had evidently been pacing up and
down, hands on hips, half-dressed and in no
gentle temper. The men and women who had
been no more than humps on the floor when
she had crept out, were now sitting up or
propped up on their elbows, sleepy-eyed and
huddled in skins and furs.

Leowulf moved first. He crossed the room in
a few strides, grasped her arms and hauled her
to her feet. 'What in the name of all that's holy
are you doing?' he demanded, shaking her.
'Why are you——?'

Adela pulled sharply away. 'Let me go,
Saxon! I have been shaken near to death this
night and I want no more of it!' He released her
abruptly and immediately his attention was
caught by the figure in the doorway.
'What——?' His hand went instinctively to the
knife in his belt, but he remembered his state of
undress and clenched his fist in impotent outrage instead.

'Leowulf,' she began, clutching his arm, ''tis
Guy de Brec——'

'Yea, *wife*, that I know,' he said pointedly in
French. 'Why is he here?'

'He came to take me back to Erinwald,
but——'

'And you have come back here?' he
enquired with cold suspicion. 'Why? Is there
something you have forgotten?'

She made an impatient gesture. 'There is no time for mockery, Saxon. My uncle and a host of his men are on their way here to burn this place to the ground, and you and everyone else in it! You must *do* something! Prepare yourselves.'

Leowulf caught her arm, his gaze searching hers, as if looking for evidence of a lie. Then: 'You came back to warn us? Why?'

'You are the most mistrustful man——' She broke off with an exasperated sigh. 'Because I do not like butchery, *that* is why I warn you.' And then, on an impulse, moved close to him and dug her fingers into his arms. 'Please hurry,' she said softly, but with a note of urgency in her voice, 'I will explain everything later.'

He gave her a hard, searching look and then nodded briefly, and turned from her to face the others. 'Up with you, Saxons! De Lise and his men are coming here to burn us out. I would avoid a fight with them if 'tis at all possible, but we must be ready for them.'

There was an instant's stunned silence as this sank in, and then the hall burst into life as, half-dressed but wide awake, the Saxons scrambled to their feet and began making preparations for an attack, something in which those men that had been with Leowulf since he left Erinwald were evidently well practised. Leowulf himself turned to Adela. 'I am very grateful to you,' he said formally. 'Now you had best be gone.' He raised his eyes and looked beyond her at Guy, still standing in the doorway. 'Take her to safety and go quickly.'

'No!' She drew back, and looked up at Leowulf, her eyes gleaming and her mouth set in a stubborn line. Did he not understand? 'I am not leaving. Guy may go if he wishes, but I will not. You may need me to prevent my uncle——'

'You think I cannot stay de Lise without you, halfling? You, who have no more substance than a river reed?'

She pulled a face and shrugged her shoulders. 'I am staying here. And you have no time,' she added quickly as he took a step towards her, 'to waste on argument with me.' He glared at her for a long moment and muttered something inaudible in his own language.

In the silence between them, Guy moved from the doorway, came into the hall and closed the door behind him. Leowulf glanced at him, and then back at Adela and finally he sighed. 'Very well, then,' he growled grudgingly, only the gruffness of his voice betraying him. 'But make yourself useful. Gather the women and babes and take them to one of the outbuildings—the stable. 'Tis biggest and furthest from the direction they will come. And *stay* there with them.'

She looked mutinous, but nodded, and with a brief, half-apologetic, half-grateful glance at

Guy moved away to do as he asked, trying to quell the thumping of her heart, and the tremors of fear stirring the pit of her stomach. If something should happen to him.... But she must not think of such things.

She moved swiftly, helping the women dress the children and hurrying them as much as she could, aware of their sidelong glances and wondering looks; and with the help of Frida and Edith, she ushered them all outside and led the disordered group into the stables. There, alert for the sound of horsemen, she impressed upon them the need for quiet, and saw most of them settled on mounds of hay and the furs they had brought with them, and then she drew Frida aside.

'See that they stay here, Frida, and try to keep the babes quiet ... And do not panic the horses.'

'But——'

Adela, however, did not stay to hear the Saxon girl's arguments. She went quickly back through the shadows to the main building, and slipped in through the door as one of the Saxons came out. Most of the men were, by now, dressed and buckling belts and rummaging amongst pallets and skins for their 'seax'. She could not see Leowulf, nor Guy, but as she began to cross the hall towards the curtained doorway, the latter caught her arm. 'He told you to stay with the other women,' he said. 'What are you doing here?'

'I am going to stay with him,' she said defiantly. 'I want Uncle Edward to see me at his side and to know that I love him and would die with him. How else is a carnage to be prevented? Our Normans have far superior weapons and far more experience in killing——'

'That I doubt,' he interrupted curtly.

'Hush. It matters not if you doubt it. Left to their own devices, these people would be slain, and all for the lies Marguerite has told and the mistakes of my uncle. I will not allow it to happen.'

He was silent for a moment, and then, slowly: 'I am here, Adela, but I will not fight Edward for the sake of this Saxon, whether or not he is your husband.'

She looked up at him and smiled a little. 'None here would ask it of you, Guy. All *I* ask is that you do not draw your sword against us.'

He shook his head, noting that she included herself as one of the Saxons with an ease that said far more about her state of mind than any protestation of love he had heard from her before. He released her, and she squeezed her arm, turning away and almost immediately forgetting about him.

She found Leowulf in his bedchamber, dressed, and sitting on the coffer at the end of the bed, turning his knife over and over in his hands; he looked up as she came in and frowned. 'Do you *ever* do as you are bid?'

'I must speak with you,' she said, moving into the room and ignoring his question. 'I must explain why my uncle is doing this. Guy has made me see the reason, and though I cannot forgive him his dishonesty, I can understand it and I want you to understand also....

'I do not wish to hear your excuses for the treachery of a nobleman and a King.'

'I cannot excuse the actions of my uncle,' she said quietly, 'but you do the King an injustice. My uncle has not been to him. He knows nothing of this.'

Leowulf narrowed his eyes, and then gave a harsh snort of laughter. 'Indeed I was a fool to believe I could trust any Norman! This has been an ill-wrought venture from the start.'

She leaned back against the closed door. 'Nay, my lord, it was a commendable thing to try to do,' she said and added, with a brief smile, 'Though I misliked your methods. But my uncle cannot afford to be out of favour with the King. He should not have allowed you to leave Erinwald as he did. You have caused such trouble since then, but the King has been away, and also perhaps too busy with other things to give his attention to it. But now, if my uncle went to him and brought to his notice that he did not make you bow to his rule when he should have done in the beginning, and has to tell him that you have now abducted his wife and niece and are demanding such terms....' She broke off, with a gesture of helplessness.

'You see how it would be? You have made my uncle look a fool. I do not excuse him. I merely wish you to understand.'

Leowulf looked at her steadily. 'He can have very little love for you or, indeed, for his wife to put you both at such risk merely that he might not look a fool.'

She said nothing for a moment, and then abruptly changed the subject, for she did not wish to think of that. 'Does your wound still pain you?'

He shook his head. ''Tis nothing. Adela, I...' He seemed to have some difficulty with what he wanted to say and eventually sighed and said, 'I would have you know that I will hold you to nothing. William will surely have the marriage annulled in the circumstances and you will be free.' He paused for a moment and studied the tips of his boots. 'This has not come about at all the way it was planned in the beginning. 'Tis a pity. I am. . . .' He made a deprecating gesture. 'I am grown quite fond of you, little one.'

She held her breath and said softly, 'Indeed, my lord?'

'I am a fool,' he said. 'There was no time for gentle courtship. I believed that by marrying you, I could make you love me and that in time you would be happy with me and forget about de Brec. It shames me that I am capable of such vanity.'

'Leowulf...' She waited until he looked up

at her, and there was, for the briefest moment,
an expression in his eyes that dispelled any last
doubts she might have had. He reminded her,
for a moment, of little Ewen. Then, feeling a
rush of warmth through her veins, she came
forward and knelt before him. 'I do not want to
leave you. I do not want our marriage annulled.
I——'

She broke off as the door was thrown open
and Olwyn stood on the threshold. He did not
need to speak. Leowulf stood up immediately,
thrusting his seax into his belt, and lifting Adela
to her feet, he held her hard against him for a
moment, kissed the top of her head and
released her.

At the door he turned to look at her, and
with a touch of humour that surprised her at
such a time, he said, 'I suppose 'tis useless to
bid you remain here, so you had best come.' He
put his arm across Olwyn's shoulder and left
her to follow them as they strode down the
passageway into the hall.

Someone fell into step beside him and gave
him the heavy two-handed axe, and although
he took it with a brief nod, at the door he
checked and with a fleeting glance at Adela,
stood it against the wall and left it there.

As he did so, a thunder of hooves outside
heralded the arrival of Adela's uncle, and the
Saxons poured outside after Leowulf and
Adela found herself standing alone in the hall,
her heart pounding and her mouth dry with

fear. She avoided looking at the axe and went to join Guy in the doorway.

Her uncle sat astride his horse, with a score of men around him, half of them carrying burning torches. They seemed somewhat at a loss to find themselves expected, and with Leowulf standing immovably with his band of rather ragged-looking Saxons defending their make-shift home, Adela felt a sudden, absurd desire to laugh. It was, however, far from amusing, and as her uncle moved his horse a few paces forward, she walked, silent and unseen, around the Saxons until she stood in the open space between Saxon and Norman, a little way from both. Her uncle looked at her, and then at Guy as he came to stand beside her.

'What is this, Guy?' he demanded angrily. 'You failed——'

'Nay, seigneur, but——'

'What do you want here, Edward de Lise?' demanded Leowulf wrathfully, in his native language. 'I have no time for idle talk with a man whose word is meaningless.'

Adela cringed, knowing that her uncle's command of the Saxon tongue was good enough that he would not mistake Leowulf's meaning. She did not know when she had last seen him so angry. He sprang to the ground, sword in hand, and took several strides towards Leowulf.

'Adela, come here,' her uncle commanded. 'Guy—fetch your horses.'

'The Lady Adela has chosen to stay,' Leowulf said quietly, drawing his seax gently from his belt and still speaking his own language. 'De Brec is free to return with you whence you came.'

At that moment one of de Lise's youthful retainers lost his head and, impatient for a fight, hurled his burning torch over the heads of the Saxons into the open doorway. It landed on the floor just inside, and the rushes blazed instantly into flames.

There was uproar. Several of the Saxons ran inside and began frantically beating out the flames; others rushed at the mounted Normans and pulled them from their horses; burning torches flew through the air. Leowulf shouted an angry command to his men, and had to repeat it with considerable abuse before they obeyed him and fell back. Adela moved swiftly to his side. 'Uncle Edward, this is absurd. Anything Marguerite has told you about our mistreatment is untrue. And I—I am wed to Leowulf.'

A mixture of expressions passed fleetingly across her uncle's face. 'What?' he spluttered. 'What are you saying? Do not play foolish games with me, Adela!'

'This is no game, uncle. 'Tis the truth. I am wed to Leowulf. And I am sorry if you do not like it, but 'tis your doing. You sent Alain to tell us that the King had agreed to the terms, that he agreed to a marriage. And the marriage has taken place.'

Sir Edward turned a murderous gaze towards the Saxon, his face turning purple with rage. 'Marguerite—she—she said nothing of this——'

'She did not know of it. But I think she said far too much, and most of it untrue.'

'Your wife is a liar and a fool,' Leowulf interrupted, this time in French. 'And no credit to you.'

'You filthy cur!' The words exploded from de Lise in a furious splutter. 'How dare you——' His sword scraped from its sheath and Leowulf took a step backwards, his knife in his hand. There was anger and hatred in both their faces.

'Nay!' Adela's sudden, anguished cry arrested their movements and she threw herself between the two men. 'You cannot do this! Are you both so blind? So stupid? What is to be gained by this?' She turned to Leowulf, a desperate, imploring look in her eyes. 'Leowulf, my lord, whatever he has done, he is my uncle and if you kill him how shall I ever forgive you? And—and who, then, will speak for you to the King? Or have you so soon forgotten why all this has happened? All is not yet lost.'

She held the Saxon's gaze for a moment, before turning her eyes on Sir Edward. 'And you, my uncle, I am ashamed to own you as my kin. What if you slay Leowulf? He is my husband and I love him,' she declared defiantly, and moved slightly so that she stood protectively in front of the Saxon and challenged her uncle. 'Would you slay me too? For what use——?'

Leowulf thrust her aside irritably. 'Get away, woman! Think you I need your protection?'

She turned and looked at him through a mist of tears. 'Nay, my lord, but I need you, and what use are you to me dead?'

There was silence; a long silence not only between Adela and Leowulf, and Leowulf and Sir Edward, but between all the Normans and Saxons. Adela turned, on an impulse, to face the men that stood hostile and protective in front of the makeshift building, and in their language, in a voice full of emotion, she said: 'Please, all of you, are you willing to give these Normans your hospitality whilst my uncle and Le—my husband discuss what is to be done?'

They all shifted uncomfortably, hostile and unwilling, yet most of them moved by the desperation in her voice and the helplessness of her position. Leowulf, frowning a displeasure she understood as disapproval that she, a woman, was interfering in something that was essentially men's business, took her arm, forcing her to look up at him.

'Go back to the other women, Adela. This is for us to settle.'

'Wait,' Sir Edward interrupted. 'I...' He looked rather embarrassed. 'Perhaps some agreement *can* be reached. The—position is somewhat altered now....' He looked at Adela, with an expression she interpreted as something between accusation and disappointment in her. She found nothing she could construe as compassion.

Leowulf looked at him for a long moment, his blue eyes flint-hard and unyielding. Adela touched his arm. 'Please, my lord,' she murmured.

He glanced down at her and frowned. Then, with a sigh, he thrust his knife back into his belt and stepped aside, bowed slightly and nodded towards the door.

They made quite a procession trooping inside. The Saxons moved back to let Sir Edward through; Leowulf followed with his hand on Adela's shoulder; Olwyn and Guy and the Saxons fell in behind them, leaving the rest of Sir Edward's men to follow.

CHAPTER
ELEVEN

THEY talked well into the early hours of the morning, closeted in Leowulf's bedchamber. Adela fetched the women from the sanctuary of the stable, and, reassuring their fears, suggested that those of them with children settled their offspring as best they could in the very limited space of the second bedchamber; the rest of the women she set to providing what food there was for those who wanted it, and sleeping space for those who did not. Olwyn and Guy she bullied into staying unobtrusively 'on guard' in the hall, for tempers ran high, rather than sitting in on the discussions taking place in Leowulf's chamber where, she said, since neither of them could speak a dozen words of the other's language, they would be more in the way than useful. 'You will serve everyone far better in here,' she said firmly.

As she went past them, Guy remarked wryly, 'You were born to arrange things, Adela. May God help the Saxon!' She merely smiled fleetingly at him and did not reply; there were other things on her mind.

Her uncle was not an easy man to pacify or divert from his course, and Leowulf was deliberately taciturn. So Adela took matters into her own hands, told both men that a lot of explaining had to be done to clear the air between them, and launched into an account of everything that had happened to her in the few days since her abrupt departure from Erinwald.

She concluded, blushingly, by telling how, without realising it, she had come to love the Saxon; how their somewhat furtive marriage had taken place and how—this, turning crimson and with a shy glance towards Leowulf—she had lain in bed wondering if he would come to her. And then Guy had come....

Sir Edward questioned her closely and rather sharply, for the most part about her feelings for the Saxon, and with rather cruel irony, demanded whether she would come to her senses if Leowulf were condemned to a life of exile. Adela merely replied that as his wife she knew where her duty lay and would go with him. It would change nothing.

Then he turned to Leowulf and demanded, gruffly, what he had to say for himself. Until now, he had seemed quite content to listen to Adela blushingly confessing her love for him, but now he looked steadily at Sir Edward for a long, disconcerting moment. Then he looked at Adela, his expression softening imperceptibly, and held out his arm to her. She went to him gladly and stood held in the circle of his arm

while he told her uncle that provided she
wanted to stay with him, he would protect her
with his life, whatever William's decision.

'For know this, Edward de Lise,' he continued grimly, 'despite your treachery I will still
go to William. For Adela's sake. But this time I
will trust no one else to smooth my path. I will
go directly to him myself, as I should have done
in the beginning.' He paused, and Adela felt
the pressure of his hand at her waist increase
slightly. 'I would like to know, de Lise, that
should any ... "mishap" befall me, she will
always find a home with you.'

'Naturally,' he said stiffly. 'Leave us, Adela,
please.'

Refusal sprang to her lips, but she turned
first to Leowulf, silently seeking his support.
He, however, said only, 'Yea, leave us, little
one, and get some sleep. This has been a long
day.'

She was about to argue with him, but caught
the twinkle in his blue eyes and the slight quirk
of his mouth, and knew that he would not be
long in joining her.

She went disconsolately from the room, and
wandered into the hall. The floor was crowded
with sleeping bodies, and a group of Saxons
had gathered by the fire and were talking
quietly. Edith and Olwyn were with them, and
she picked her way carefully across to them and
sat down beside them on the skins which had
been spread on the rushes. She answered their

questions about what was happening carefully, and settled down to wait, forcing herself not to look round at the curtained doorway every few moments.

When Leowulf eventually emerged with his mantle across his arm, she was sitting with her knees pulled up, and her arms lying across them as a rest for her head; she was drowsy but not quite asleep and when he touched her arm, she was awake instantly. He helped her to her feet and murmured, 'Come,' and led her to the door and outside, and holding her close to his side against the cold night air. They went to the stable, where several skins and furs still covered the hay and there spent the rest of the night, curled up together beneath his mantle.

'Your uncle has decided to accompany me to William,' he told her softly.

She raised her head from his shoulder and tried to make out his features in the darkness. 'Why?'

'For your sake. He accepts that we are wed, but would not have you spend your life in exile. He will speak to William and vouch for my ... "conduct" and sincerity.' He paused and kissed her forehead as she lay at his side. 'We have decided that we must go as soon as possible, little one. As soon as it is light we will all go to Erinwald, for it will be easier to protect one building with a few men. From there, your uncle and I and some others will go to William.'

'So soon?' There was disappointment in her voice. 'But ... we will be so tired, and it is not an easy journey, nor a short one. Can we not go to Erinwald tomorrow and to the King the day after?'

'Nay. Think, Adela, how crowded Erinwald will be with so many. Tempers will run high and both Saxon and Norman will claim it theirs. And if William agrees that Erinwald is mine, your uncle will have to have some other place to live—the sooner 'tis done, the better. For us, too.' He pulled her closer to him. 'Are you still so sure you want whatever life I can give you? It may not be a good life, nor an easy one. And you have said you wished to return to Normandy.'

She smiled in the darkness. 'That was before. I think perhaps I can survive in this primitive land with its unschooled barbarians for a little longer.'

'You are insolent, wench, and I think I must teach you to have better respect your elders!'

'Yea, my lord,' she said with a secret smile, sensing he was torn between the desire for sleep, for which his body ached, and the need he felt to make her truly his wife. 'But not tonight,' she added softly, 'you are tired and your wound is not full-healed, and tomorrow will be another long day. I am bone-weary and will sleep like a babe.'

She snuggled up against him, hearing his soft

chuckle and the gentle pressure of his hand on her waist as he held her close, and was well satisfied.

The following day dawned bright, clear and cold with frost sparkling on the ground. Attempting to gather everyone and everything together and organise the return to Erinwald proved more than a little harassing. It was early and because most had retired late, tempers were easily frayed and children fractious, and there was still animosity and mistrust between Saxon and Norman. Belongings and food were loaded into a cart and as there were not enough horses to go round, some had to double up and some babies and children rode in the cart. The priest had been prevailed upon to remain with them for a little while, and had undertaken to marry Olwyn and Edith as soon as things were settled.

Eventually, with the morning further advanced than they would have liked, the motley procession set off, and it seemed to Adela that the journey took twice as long as it had done when they had been snatched from Erinwald, and then it had been dark.

However, after several stoppages to allow stragglers to catch up, and one mishap when the cart overturned and spilled its load of stores, children and women into a chaotic heap in the road, they finally came to Erinwald.

Marguerite came running out to greet what

she obviously assumed to be a victorious return, but with concern on her face.

'Edward! Guy and Adela have not——' She broke off and stopped abruptly as she saw her niece and Guy, and the mixture of expressions that crossed her face as her gaze travelled from Leowulf to the hapless cart, back over the odd mixture of Norman and Saxon, of men, women, children, dogs and a priest, delighted Adela considerably, and quite overcame the anger and accusations she had been nursing on the journey to confront her aunt with.

For the first time Adela saw her uncle stern with his wife. What was said between them in private later she never knew, but he explained the situation in as few words as possible and made it quite clear in front of all of them that while he was away, he expected every Saxon to be treated with as much respect and consideration as any other guest. The news that Adela and Leowulf were already wed obviously horrified Marguerite, but she made no comment and merely bowed her head and asked, as she surveyed the two-score and more people, just where everyone was to be housed, and for how long.

'We go today,' he said, dismounting and signalling everyone else to do the same. 'Leowulf and myself and twelve men, six Saxons, six Normans. The rest remain. We should not be gone much longer than a week.' He gave a few swift orders to several of his men about the horses and stores and led the way inside.

Adela, at her husband's side, watched his face as they stepped into the home he had left so many months ago, and the softening of his features and the deepening colour of his blue eyes brought home to her again how little she knew of him. It seemed strange that such a man, a 'lion' among the Saxons, could have such tender feelings towards a building none could describe as beautiful. And yet she understood it and loved him more because of it.

The next hours passed quickly, too quickly for Adela, because until then she had naturally assumed that she would be going with her husband. But as she led him into her chamber and began to gather together the clothing and oddments she would need, and put them with his, he stopped her, and drew her towards him.

'Nay, little one. You must stay here.'

She shook her head. 'I am coming with you.'

He sighed and for a few moments stared at the wall beyond her. 'There is nothing I would like more,' he answered, 'than to have you at my side. But I want you safe, and who knows what will happen at William's court? I have wrought much damage here since he took Harold's life and crown, and he may think it safer to——'

'No!' She cut across his words with fear in her voice. 'No, I will not listen. William is a hard man but a fair one, and my uncle is close to him.

If he vouches for you, and if the King sees that he trusts you enough to have allowed his niece to wed you, he will accept you as a subject and give Erinwald back. And all the other reasons you gave me before——'

'Yea, but it changes nothing. You must stay. To keep peace here if for no other reason. You are loved by Saxon and Norman, you speak both languages easily, and as my wife and de Lise's niece you command respect. Marguerite,' he dismissed her with an impatient gesture, 'is useless, and if she thinks she is to be ousted from here will not be inclined to act as she should.'

She pulled away from him, walked across to the shuttered window and turned back to face him. 'I am afraid that if you go without me, something may happen to you, something that may prevent you getting back to me. I will not be able to survive a week knowing nothing and worrying. I *must* come.'

'Adela,' he said sharply, 'I do not want a struggle with you over this. You will do as I say.'

Startled that he could be so sharp with her, a lump rose involuntarily in her throat and brought tears to her eyes. She was very still and silent, unaware that she looked like a rebuked child, and after a moment he sank down on to the bed and, sighing heavily he looked across at her and said, 'Forgive me, I did not mean to speak so harshly.'

She was instantly contrite. His voice sounded heavy and weary, and now that she looked at him properly she could see lines of strain and tiredness around his eyes. She had forgotten his wounded shoulder, forgotten that all the responsibility and the decisions were his ... She crossed the room quickly and knelt down before him, drawing his head to hers and kissing his forehead. 'I am selfish and thoughtless, and I doubt that I will ever be a credit to you,' she murmured, looking into his blue eyes. 'I will stay, and pray for you every day.'

He put his arms around her and held her tight and they remained thus, saying nothing until Adela shifted slightly to ease the cramp in her knees. Then he raised his head and said, 'I would take Olwyn with me, unless you would feel safer to have him here with you. You know de Brec comes with us?'

She nodded. 'Yes, because of Isabelle. But Olwyn is a good man and a good friend. You will need him with you. We shall be well guarded here and I can help Edith prepare for her wedding.' Then, with a sigh, she drew herself to her feet and out of the circle of his arms. 'Come, try to sleep for a little while; no one can set off until the horses are rested.'

Leaving him to sleep, she went in search of Marguerite, who was somewhat subdued, and between them they contrived to put the household into some sort of order, and with a few harsh words between them.

In the end, the departure was left until the following morning after all, for by the time the horses were rested and fed and the men had eaten and were packed and ready, it was little more than an hour to darkness, and to set off in dusk would have been folly.

It gave Adela a valuable extra night with her husband, but they talked for a little while of a future at Erinwald, with no mention that there might be some other outcome to this interview with William. Then they fell asleep, both of them weary and exhausted. When the time came to see them off the following morning, she could not help but wish they had gone the night before. There was too much time; too much time for worry and fear, for restraining herself from begging to go too and for regretting that they had fallen asleep in each other's arms before their soft words and gentle kisses had led them to a consummation of their marriage.

The actual parting was swift and a little formal, and apart from a moment when she clung hard to him and swallowed down the lump in her throat, she managed to maintain a commendable control over her emotions.

Then they were gone, and for the next few days, Adela plunged into a fervour of activity, resolutely forcing all fears and anxieties about him to the back of her mind. Erinwald was swept, scrubbed, dusted and cleaned, from back to front and from top to bottom. Furs, skins and tapestries were taken up, brushed, shaken, beaten and put back. Rushes were turned or replaced, and anything that needed mending or stitching had her calling for anyone who was not otherwise occupied. The stables and outbuildings were swept and the kitchens scrubbed. No small corner escaped.

Marguerite was not so insensitive that she did not realise Adela's need to occupy herself, so she made no objections, and indeed was well aware of the danger her own husband was in if the King became aware of just how he had handled the whole affair and took exception to it. She did not trust Leowulf to hold silent about it, and had lost none of her dislike of him with the knowledge that Adela had married him and was apparently more than happy with a man she considered no more than a barbarian. She forbore, however, to remind Adela that Leowulf's success on this mission would mean that she and Sir Edward would be dependent upon William's goodwill for another home in England.

The week was the longest Adela had ever lived through and when the week dragged into eight and then nine days, she grew frantic. A feast had been prepared and wanted only the last-minute touches, and she despaired that all might go to waste, and food was not so plentiful at this time of year that they could afford that.

She tried desperately to quell her fears and act as if she were quite calm and unworried, for she was well aware of the effect the state of her own nerves was having on Edith and Marguerite. It was a wonder the gown they made for Edith's wedding turned out as well as it did. Adela felt no uncertainty about what she would do were Leowulf forced to live a life of exile in the hills, or flee north. She would go with him. Her fears were for the multitude of things that could happen to him whilst he was at William's mercy; for the possibility that he might not return at all. At least once an hour she looked up at the sky and prayed that it would not snow.

CHAPTER
TWELVE

IT was the afternoon of the eleventh day. Adela wandered listlessly outside, wrapped in a heavy mantle against the cold and determined to walk away at least one of the intolerably slow-passing hours and ease a little of the sick anxiety churning her stomach. If only there were some way of hearing news, if only she knew what the King had decided. The woods were stark and black against the heavy grey-ness of a sky which held a threatening possi-bility of snow. She closed her eyes briefly and prayed that it would not come.

She walked a little way, staring unseeingly at the frozen ground and letting her thoughts drift idly on the events of the past few days, trying to draw some reassurance from them.

'Adela.'

She looked up, startled, and suddenly the anxious expression on her face was lifted and relief and excitement sparkled in her eyes. 'Guy!' she looked instinctively beyond him, wondering, searching for the others, for Leowulf; trembling, her heart pounding pain-fully in anticipation. 'Where are the rest?

What happened...? Did the King—where is Leowulf?'

A dozen questions flew into her head and she did not know which to ask first. But Guy de Brec was silent, and alone, and she drew her gaze back to his, and swallowed down the constriction in her throat. Only now she took in his appearance and the obvious signs of a hard ride; the greyness of his face, the lines of weariness and the grim set of his mouth; and the dark, ominous stain on his tunic.

'You—are wounded?' She forced out the words, her mouth dry and a sick, choking dread in the pit of her stomach.

He shook his head. ' 'Tis nothing.' He paused and then, 'Adela, I have ill news.'

She drew a long breath. 'Tell me, then, and quickly,' she said quietly, her eyes fixed on his face. 'Is he——'

'He was to have been hanged, but he fled and is now hiding some distance from here. You must come with me, Adela, and as soon as possible, for I am but a day's ride ahead of Sir Edward, who comes in search of him to put him to the sword in William's name.'

She stared at him, horrified. 'And you were wounded helping his escape?'

'Yes, but 'tis well enough. We must hasten. Can you get food and clothing out without being seen? No one must know, Adela. Not even Marguerite.'

She nodded, understanding the need for

such secrecy, and her heart throbbing with anxiety. 'Is my lord hurt?'

Guy shook his head and urged her to hurry, adding a caution to be careful. 'I will take my horse to the stream for water and then wait for you here.'

She nodded, and turning quickly, made her way back to Erinwald, slowing abruptly as she came in sight of it so that any who saw her might think she merely returned from her walk. Frida was in her chamber examining the cloth they were to have made into a new gown, and Adela decided that if she were to succeed in leaving Erinwald without arousing suspicion, she must trust one person at least to help her. There was none she trusted more than Frida.

Briefly she told her what Guy had said to her, and enlisted her aid in secreting food from the kitchen and something for his wound from her box. Wide-eyed and obedient, the Saxon girl went to do as she was bid and Adela set about collecting the merest necessities of clothing and other basic items they would need. She also took a small knife. When Frida returned a little while later, swearing she had not been noticed, she put everything into the smallest bundle she could make up and donned her warmest clothing.

Managing, somehow, to appear as if they had been sorting out her chamber and were removing a bundle of unwanted things, they contrived to safely reach the outside of the building without arousing any undue comment. She took her leave of Frida, who was sworn to secrecy, and after toying briefly with the idea of attempting to get a horse, she abandoned it as too great a risk and slipped quickly into the cover of the trees.

Guy was waiting, and after securing her bundle on to the saddle, took her up before him and set off away from Erinwald. The trees around Erinwald were sparser than the woods around Leowulf's hideout in the hills had been, but they afforded some cover until they were out of sight of the building. They travelled the first few miles quickly, to put as great a distance between themselves and Erinwald as possible before darkness or bad weather stopped them.

They went for the most part in silence. She asked one or two questions about what had happened but he seemed unwilling to talk, concentrating on riding as fast as possible without over-tiring the horse or setting them all in a ditch. He said they had some way to go, but thought they would be there by nightfall if it did not snow. She suggested they stop so that she might attend to his wound, but he refused and said there would be time enough for that later.

She thought that perhaps he was concerned that he was aiding her escape to a man her uncle must kill, and she wondered what would happen to him were it discovered. All he would

say in answer to that was that Edward thought
him at William's court still, with Isabelle, and
would not know of his part in her disappearance.

She lapsed into silence to dwell on thoughts
of a life with Leowulf of necessity now in hiding, and wondered where they could go to be
safe. Merely the thought of being with him
lifted her spirits away from the acute disappointment that he had not been treated more
leniently by William.

Dusk fell, and Guy pressed on, and the light
had all but failed when they turned off the road
and headed towards a small shadowy building a
little way up a narrow track. The building was
in darkness as they drew to a halt outside. 'Is
this the place?' she asked as he lifted her down.
'Is Leowulf here?'

'Go in,' he said, and led his horse round to
the rear of the building. She went inside, but
could see nothing for the darkness, and when
she called Leowulf's name softly, she was
answered only by silence.

Guy came in with their bundles and set to
work to light one of the torches in the wall-
sconce. He had some difficulty, but eventually
shadows chased across the floor and Adela was
able to look round. There was a look and a
smell of long disuse about the place. 'Is there
no one here?' she demanded.

He shook his head. 'The Saxons fled when
we came here on our way to take Erinwald. It

was too small and worthless for us to waste time with—but the Saxons never returned.'

'And Leowulf?'

He was silent for a moment and then walked across to her. 'Come, forget the Saxon.'

He took her into his arms and before she could prevent it, had kissed her clumsily. With a startled cry, she tried to twist herself free and as she did so caused him to slip on the unsavoury rushes rotting on the floor, and they both crashed to the ground. In her haste to be free of him, she thrust her hand hard against his chest, in the place where his tunic was stiff with dried blood, pushed herself away and scrambled to her feet. It struck her like cold water to her addled wits: he was wounded and he had not even flinched! She had not even felt a dressing. And Leowulf was certainly not here....

She stood away from him, wide-eyed, as he picked himself up from the floor. 'Why have you brought me here?' she demanded. 'You are not wounded! Why did you lie to me? And where is Leowulf?'

'Leowulf?' He turned a bench upright and sat down upon it. 'Come, sit down.' She did not move and he sighed and said quietly: 'Very well. Adela, Leowulf is dead. He was hanged on William's orders.'

For a moment everything within her seemed suddenly to be still. It could not be true. Slowly, she shook her head.

Guy went on: 'Your uncle believed you would be in danger from the Saxons when they learned of it, and had me hasten on ahead to take you to safety. The lies were necessary so that you would tell no one—it would have been difficult to get away had you been stricken with grief.'

She remained silent. She did not know what to think or say. She did not want to believe him. 'Is it true, Guy? Truly he is dead?'

He nodded. 'It is true. I am sorry, Adela.'

She stood motionless, expressionless, unable to react to what he had said although his words kept repeating themselves over and over in her mind. Leowulf dead? She stared at the floor, swallowing a painful lump in her throat. Surely it could not be true. And yet it had the ring of truth. And Guy would not deliberately be so cruel to her, surely. He had lied to her before, but he had explained the need of it. How could she not believe him? Her uncle would wish her in Normandy, certainly, for she had declared her love for a Saxon heathen and been wed to him, and then William had declared him traitor and had him hanged. A shudder of horror went through her.

She tried to speak but no words would come, and suddenly she found herself gasping for air, drawing long, rasping breaths that could not pass the obstruction in her throat.

'Adela!' Guy moved swiftly forward, took her arms and shook her. With a choked cry the lump in her throat dissolved and a solitary tear slid silently down her face.

He released her and after a moment or two she recovered sufficiently to say tremulously, 'Where—where are you taking me?'

'To Normandy. You will be safe there.'

She put her hand to her temples, trying to clear her head sufficiently to think clearly. 'I would have been safe at Erinwald, Guy.' She raised her eyes, full of pain and bewilderment, and looked at him. 'Take me back to Erinwald.'

He shook his head. 'I cannot. There is nothing there for you now.' He walked across to the bundles he had left lying near the door and picked them up. 'We must go on again as soon as it is light,' he said, holding out the bundle that was hers. 'You must rest. Do you wish to eat?'

She shook her head. How could she eat? Feeling numb and quite unlike herself, she took the bundle from him and forced herself to walk across to the far side of the hall, in the gloomy shadows. There was another bench, and she brushed the dirt and dust from it and lay down, using the clothes to rest her head upon and wrapping her mantle tightly around her against the cold.

Leowulf was dead and she felt only a cold numbness. She was waiting for the full force of it to hit her, and crush her; but there was only blankness. She stared into the gloomy, uncertain half-light and felt only a seeping misery

overcome her. How long she lay there she did
not know, but she was aroused by Guy asking if
she slept. 'How can I sleep?' she murmured.

'Then come and warm yourself—I have
made a fire of sorts.'

She allowed him to help her up and made no
struggle when he put his arm about her and led
her to the bench he had drawn close to the fire.
'Adela, forget the Saxon,' he said again. 'How
could you love an unshaven heathen with no
manners and a fondness for the barbaric? You
scarce knew him long enough to——'

She turned on him angrily. 'How dare you
speak thus of him? 'Tis no——'

'Nay, Adela,' he interrupted, 'do not be
angry. Listen to me.' And she subsided, turning
to stare into the flames. If Leowulf were dead,
what did it matter if such as Guy said harsh
things of him? 'I have ever been more than
fond of you, Adela, and when I thought I had
lost you to the Saxon, I knew I loved you——'

She was uncomfortably aware of his arm
around her and turned to face him. 'How can
you speak to me of love now?' she cried unhappily. 'And with such pretty words! And what of
Isabelle?'

'Isabelle?' She did not like the sneer on his
face as he said it and began to feel rather
uneasy. 'The Lady Isabelle is certainly very
beautiful, and I must wed her.' He shrugged his
shoulders. 'She is very wealthy and will bring
me far more than you would have done, sweet

Adela, and she has many friends at William's court and indeed has some kinship with William himself.'

She turned away, disgusted. 'How hard and scheming you are!'

'But it is you I love, Adela. I will take you to Normandy and see you safe with the Sisters at La Roche—and when I have been released from my duty to your uncle and have wed the fair Isabelle, I shall take her to my home and set about begetting many sons. You and I will be but a few miles apart then, and I can easily spend whole days with you—Isabelle will be far too occupied with the coming of her off-spring.'

She turned her head slowly to look at him, scarcely able to believe what she had heard, stunned by the crude, cruel way he was speaking and sick with disgust. 'Do you realise what you are saying?' she asked incredulously.

He made no reply, and she gave a little harsh laugh. 'Oh, no, Guy, I shall not go to La Roche. There is less for me in Normandy than there is at Erinwald with my uncle, and I shall not be cloistered in La Roche for your amusement!'

'Not for my amusement, Adela, for my pleasure.' He took hold of her wrist before she could draw her hand away, and held it tightly, leaning over and kissing her neck. She shivered involuntarily and tried to pull away. 'You *will* go to La Roche, my pretty. I have wanted you so much, though God knows I tried not to.

Isabelle is beautiful, but she has not your spirit, your fire. It is you, Adela, you.'

Again he bent to kiss her neck, and she twisted away, avoiding him, yet still ensnared by his hand gripping her wrist.

'No one can keep me at La Roche against my will!' she insisted, her voice trembling a little with fear. 'My uncle——'

'Edward will never return to Normandy,' he said with a shrug. 'And how else should he hear of your plight? And consider,' he paused, and still holding her, said reflectively, 'I shall tell the Sisters that you are a close relative of mine ... Yes, the unfortunate victim of a Saxon's lust, I think, and turned quite demented by your ordeal. Then, if you should already carry the Saxon's child, 'tis explained.'

Adela grew more and more appalled with each word he spoke, unable to believe that this was the same man who had professed to love her like a sister, and having taken her from Leowulf's hideout, had then taken her back to warn him. Surely this was not the same man?

'You call Leowulf barbaric? You disgust me, Guy de Brec, you are worse than any Saxon——'

She tried desperately to wrench herself out of his grasp; she was half free, but he pulled her back, forced her to her knees before him as he sat there, and kissed her ruthlessly, bruisingly, heedless of her struggles. She forced her head aside and almost spat at him in her disgust, her

every muscle tensed and every feeling
repulsed. Then he, too, was on his knees, forcing her down. She cried out, knowing the futility of it, knowing there was no one to help her,
yet silently praying for a miracle. She fought
like a hellion, and heard only his soft laughter
in her ear and the sound of her gown tearing at
the shoulder. She felt his hand on her breast
and revulsion rose up in her; she kicked
scratched, clawed and bit, called him every
name she could think of with oaths she did not
realise she knew, and was draining herself of
strength.

And then, suddenly, he uttered a sharp cry of
pain and cursed her. For the briefest moment
she was free, and in that instant she kicked him
with all the force she had left and scrambled
away.

'You are mad!' she gasped. 'Mad, mad..!'
and she threw herself to the end of the room
and caught up her mantle and her bundle,
desperate and terribly afraid, her hands trembling as she fumbled for the knife. Her fingers
closed around its handle and she whirled round
to face him with it. 'I will kill you if you come
near me!' she threatened, her voice harsh and
quivering.

'Do not be such a fool,' he snapped impatiently. 'Come, give me the knife.'

He moved towards her with his hand out-
stretched and she backed away, the fingers of
her other hand clutching the mantle until her

knuckles turned white. He made a sudden move towards her, but she twisted away, and in another swift movement had darted across the room to the other side of a long table. She was now within reach of the door, and before he could come any closer she threw herself towards it, pulled it open and fled outside into the darkness, frantically pulling it shut behind her to delay him.

It was snowing, and snowing quite hard. Instinctively, Adela turned and ran to the back of the building—conscious of Guy behind her and knowing only that she must hide. The ground was dangerously slippery, but she had no time to be mindful of it, and threw herself into one of the smaller buildings. It had been a storehouse and in the darkness she thrust her way through all manner of unseen obstacles, stifling cries of pain as she bruised her legs on them in her haste to get as far back as she could. She wriggled deep into a jumble of coffers, sacks, boxes and discarded and broken furniture, and there squatted down, scarcely daring to breathe, every sense alert and waiting as she strained to listen for even the smallest sound.

And then she heard him outside, calling. 'Adela, do not be a fool. You cannot hope to escape me——'

Her breathing sounded horribly loud and her heart was pounding wildly. She could see nothing, but she could hear him moving about

outside, calling her name. Then he came into
the storehouse. 'Are you in here? Be sensible,
Adela. Come——' He moved a few objects
and dragged others aside; her fingers tightened
on the knife, and she squeezed her eyes tightly
closed and prayed.

Then he gave up and went outside. 'Adela,
you cannot escape,' he called. 'You will need
the horse and I shall stay very close by him.
And if you are foolish enough to try to go on
foot, in this weather you will surely die. You
have no food, and you are scarce likely to meet
anyone on the road. I shall find you, Adela,
soon enough.' He was silent a moment, then:
'But for now, you can stay where you are and
be cold, and think of your Saxon dancing at the
end of William's rope!'

He went away then, laughing, and left her.

'Oh, dear God.' Adela closed her eyes and
tears squeezed out from beneath her lashes.
She sat down properly to ease her cramped
limbs and put her face in her hands, overwhelmed by despair. She could not believe that
this was happening to her. Leowulf dead and
Guy a madman—she trapped miles from safety
in a deserted place in the snow.... It was too
much for her to bear. What had she done to
anger God so much?

Tears of misery welled up in her and she
broke down and wept, wretched and helpless.
And when she could weep no more. she dragged her mantle around her shoulders, rested

her head on her arms and thought that she was surely lost. That Guy—dear Guy who had been such a friend and comfort to her in her first days at Erinwald could now, suddenly, become so evil and make such a hideous suggestion, was such an appalling thought that she felt quite sick. And she could not doubt that he was quite capable of carrying out the awful plan. A convulsive shudder went through her at the thought of it. How could he turn on her in such a way? She could see no way out, and with Leowulf dead, did it really matter what happened to her or where she went?

But Adela had more in her than that, and she had more pride than to allow Guy to use her thus without a fight. Leowulf was dead and there was, deep within her, a nagging ache that was loss. Later she would most certainly grieve for him, and for the cruel waste of it. But there were more immediate troubles that beset her now, and Adela was not one who gave herself easily to defeat.

A picture of Frida came into her mind and jolted her with a sudden stab of hope. Guy had told her she must tell no one, but she had; she had told Frida. She had told her she was going to Leowulf. Surely, then, when Sir Edward came back to Erinwald with the news that Leowulf was dead, Frida would realise that there had been some trick and tell him that Guy had taken her away. They would come in search of her. They would not know where he had taken her, but surely they might guess that the only place he could safely take her was Normandy and there was little choice of roads south in these parts.

If her uncle did indeed think Guy still at William's court, Guy must have ridden like a demon to reach Erinwald before them. And perhaps he had not, after all, been as much as a day's ride ahead of them, as he had said. But as soon as it began to grow light Guy would be searching for her, and she knew well enough that she would not be able to escape him for very long. With the snow, every step would leave a telling footprint for him to follow. And, if the snow continued, her uncle would be further delayed and the chances of him catching up with them in time were faint. Guy was far stronger than she; she could not hope to hold him off for long, and once he had overcome her resistance it would not matter very much anyway.

Her thoughts threatened to lead her once more to despair, but she caught herself up and forced herself to concentrate on more hopeful things. She had to get to the horse. There must surely be some way to lure Guy away long enough?

She leaned back where she sat between two large coffers and several other tall, indistinguishable objects, hunching herself up against the cold and thinking longingly of the fire she had left. She had a long, cold night ahead of her to dwell upon ways and means. After a little while she lay down and curled herself up in the space where she had sat, and for a long time lay twisting various means of escape around in her mind, and finding nothing satisfactory. Yet at least it helped keep thoughts of Leowulf away. Eventually she slept somehow, but lightly and uneasily, woken frequently by discomfort and unfamiliar sounds, and upsetting dreams of Leowulf. . . .

As the darkness outside deepened into the black hour before dawn, Adela crept from her hiding place, sore and aching, and felt her way through to the doorway. It had stopped snowing, but the ground was inches deep in an even, glittering whiteness. She sat down again just inside the door, and waited.

The darkness began to lift and a greyness lightened the eastern sky. She got up and peered carefully outside, but there was no sign of Guy, and for a brief moment she felt a tremor of panic that he might have ridden off in the night and left her there to die. But she quickly dismissed the thought and set about the task ahead of her.

She ventured out and looked round with grim purpose and, with sudden hope, her gaze alighted on a dense group of trees and bushes a little way off to her right, that looked almost impenetrable. If she could but make Guy believe she had gone that way, and if it only proved impossible for him to follow her on horseback, she might have a slender chance.

She had no time to hesitate and, pulling her mantle close around her, walked purposefully towards the trees, leaving a trail of footprints. The copse was, indeed, far too thick with close-growing trees, withered wintry undergrowth and spiky, leafless shrubs to permit easy passage by horse. She bravely plunged into the daunting gloom, ensuring that her footprints were left in the muddy ground and the smattering of snow that had fallen from the trees, and that the twigs of shrubs were broken to show her passing. In a while she turned back, but this time was careful to tread where she would leave no marks, and to leave the undergrowth as undisturbed as possible.

As she came within sight of the open ground once more, she stopped abruptly with a sharp intake of breath and crouched down behind a tree. Guy was calling her name, and in another moment she could see him emerging from between the buildings. It did not take him more than a few seconds to see her trail of footprints, and within a very few moments he had fetched the horse and was riding at a trot towards her. How gullible he was! she thought bitterly, and crept nearer to the fringe of the copse, crouching lower still in the cover of a wide tree-trunk and a mass of spiky bushes.

He pulled up at the edge of the trees only a few feet from her. She did not dare raise her head for fear that the white clouds of her breath on the cold air would betray her, and instead kept her nose and mouth buried in her mantle and her head bent low. Every muscle was tense and aching but she dared not stir. She heard him curse and dismount, and after a moment's agonising silence, heard him crashing away through the trees. She let her breath out very slowly and gingerly raised her head; in another instant she was up and running.

It took only a few moments to reach the horse, another to haul herself into the saddle and yet another to turn him round and dig her heels into his flanks. But Guy heard her and as she rode away she heard him thrashing through the bare-branched shrubs, cursing her violently and viciously.

She closed her ears to the sound and set the horse at a reckless pace, until, rounding the main building and heading towards the road, the poor creature stumbled and she was nearly unseated. Then she calmed herself and drew up to a safer speed. She gained the road and turned back the way they had come, hoping that it was towards Erinwald, caring very little what became of Guy de Brec.

CHAPTER
THIRTEEN

IT began to snow again as it grew light, and
Adela had to bow her head against it and allow
the horse to pick his own way along the peril-
ously slippery road. Cold, hungry, tired and in
very low spirits, she began to wonder, a little
bitterly, whether she would perhaps have been
better advised to stay with Guy and take her
chances. As the weather worsened once more
she seriously doubted if it was at all possible for
her to find her way to Erinwald safely, especi-
ally as she had no clear idea where she was. In
these conditions, too, it was scarcely likely that
her uncle would be able to set out to search for
her, even supposing he had reached Erinwald
before the worst of the weather.

However, the thought of Guy and what he
had tried to do made her shudder; even death,
she decided, was infinitely preferable to the
ignominious fate awaiting her at Guy de Brec's
hands.

How long they pushed on doggedly along
that snow-covered, treacherous road she had
no idea. It was fully light and she was slumped
in the saddle in semi-conscious, half-frozen
desolation, ready to drop. A sudden sound

ahead of her, a shout, jerked her to her senses
and she peered through the blur of snow to
see the indistinct shapes of several horsemen
blocking the road.

Dear God, no more. The thought went
through her mind with weary detachment. She
sagged in the saddle and knew that this time she
would be unable to fight; she had no strength or
will left to resist and they must do as they would
with her and leave her to die, for she cared
nothing what happened to her now.

The centre horseman moved forward and
came towards her. He said something in curt
Saxon and she raised her head slowly. It took
her several long seconds to recognise the tall,
bearded unmistakable figure before her, and
when she did, she thought she was suffering
from delusions.

'Adela!' He brought his horse to a standstill
beside her. 'Adela....'

'Leowulf. My lord....' She swayed dangerously and would have fallen, but for his swift
movement to steady her. He leaned over and
with apparent ease lifted her up and drew her
on to his own saddle. She looked up at him, her
dark eyes bewildered and disbelieving; she
raised a trembling, ice-cold hand to touch his
face, and wonder replaced the disbelief. 'My
lord...?' she murmured. 'Is it truly you?'

'Yea, Adela, 'tis I. You are safe, little one,
quite safe.'

She could not speak for the relief and

thankfulness and joy that choked her, and was too overcome by her emotions to do more than look up at him with a smile on her face and tears pouring silently down her face.

A look, almost of agony, passed swiftly across his face and was gone, and he bent his head and kissed her fiercely, hungrily, longingly, so that she knew how deep had been his own fears of having lost her without the need for words. She clung to him, not knowing whether to laugh or cry and returning his kisses fervently.

With great difficulty, he drew away and murmured huskily, 'Come, Wycke is but a mile or two away, and a fire and food and a warm bed awaits.' He took up the reins of Adela's horse and led it back to the half-dozen men who awaited him.

'Guy,' she said, with a catch in her voice, 'Guy is back there. At a deserted place ... I took his horse and left him——'

'Hush, little one. He shall not escape.' He said a few brief words to Olwyn, who nodded assent and turned away to ride back in the direction from which Adela had come.

The little procession set off slowly through the snow. 'He said William had condemned you and you had to flee,' she told him shakily. '—I believed him, but it was a trick, and—and then he said you were dead, and I believed that also, and—and—I thought never to see you again....' She could not go on, and buried her face against his chest.

He held her close and kissed the top of her head. 'Nay, wench,' he said gently, 'I am not so easy to lose. But hush now, and we will speak of it later.'

He pressed his face against her wet hair and tightened his hold on her and she, happy in the knowledge that he was alive and well, was content enough to wait for the explanations. She slipped her arm beneath his mantle and curled it around him to hold on to his belt at the back, and leaned against him with complete and utter faith in his ability to care for her.

The place to which they went was Wycke, the sprawling, single-storey homestead from which Edith had fled many months ago when the Normans had come. Now, the 'murdering swine' that had wrought such damage had long since been withdrawn by William, and Saxons again held Wycke, in his name.

There was food and ale for those who wanted it, and dry clothes and a place to rest or sleep for all, for they had ridden through the night by the light of torches and paused at Wycke at dawn only to allow the horses to feed and rest. Adela, cold and wet and very shaken by her ordeal, was carried in by Leowulf, and although she was aware of a blur of anxious faces, she was spared any further trial and taken immediately to a private chamber.

He put her down in a chair, by a fire that crackled and blazed, and drew off her sodden mantle. In doing so, he could not fail to notice the torn shoulder of her gown and the bruises, and bending down before her, he gripped her arms unwittingly tight and demanded, in grim tones of barely-concealed anger, whether de Brec had hurt her.

She shook her head and put her hand on his arm. 'Nay, my lord, though he tried.' She lifted her eyes and managed a smile. 'You should know that I do not submit so easily.'

He chuckled and kissed her, much reassured by the bantering tone of her voice. 'Later we shall see how easily you submit, wench!' Pulling a wolf pelt from the bed he wrapped it around her, and only then turned to the girl who had followed them in with an armful of dry clothing.

She would have given the clothes over to Leowulf and gone to fetch food and mulled ale for them, but he bade her stay and see to his lady while he went to speak with his host and to fetch whatever sustenance they needed. He knew well enough what would happen if he were left to remove Adela's wet clothes, and she was in no condition for that yet.

Adela submitted gratefully to the girl's ministrations and wriggled thankfully out of her wet, torn gown to be helped into a dry one which, if not a perfect fit, was clean and warm. The girl rubbed the worst of the wetness from her hair and combed it out in front of the fire, so that when she left, the long, dark tresses were merely damp.

Leowulf soon returned with food and ale and drew up another chair to sit with her by the fire. 'You look better,' he said approvingly.

She nodded, reaching for the warm, fragrant ale he held out for her, and leaning back in the chair with a deep sigh, she sipped it appreciatively before looking up at him. 'I thought never to see you again,' she said softly, her dark eyes seeming to drink in every detail of his face.

'Nor I you, wife.' He paused, watching her sip the ale and seem to draw strength from it, and then said softly: 'Tell me.'

It was difficult for her to clear her head of the fears and horrors of the previous day and night but she did so, and abandoning her chair to kneel by his side so that she could entwine her fingers in his and feel the comfort of his arm round her waist, she began slowly to relate the story, shivering a little at some parts and unable to disguise her bewilderment that Guy should have proved himself so despicably evil, perhaps even a madman. Leowulf chuckled when she told how she had tricked Guy of his horse, and he squeezed her waist and said he had always known her for a cunning little vixen.

When she had finished, he bent over and kissed her longingly, but she, too, had ques-tions, and she drew away a little. 'What of you, my lord? Was all that Guy said nothing but lies? Did William——?'

He stopped her rush of questions with a kiss. He had other things in mind than the telling of his tale, but knew Adela would not be content until all her questions were answered.

' 'Tis no great tale,' he said. 'I made my peace with William and all turned out as it should. Your uncle and Marguerite are given new lands further south. But what a man is William!' he added with sudden animation. 'England may be lost to Saxon, but with such a man on the throne, we can build a united England without need for further bloodshed.' Then he smiled and tugged playfully at her hair. 'I bought you such presents, Adela! And so eager was I to be back in my wife's arms that we drove the horses near to exhaustion and your uncle complained greatly! But, alas! There was no welcome at Erinwald. No sweet Adela pacing the floor and wringing her hands in torment to have me home again!'

'You mock me, my lord?' she murmured with a faint smile.

'Nay, my dove, I mean only to lighten the telling of it, for I was sorely angered to find you gone and half the people of Erinwald out searching the woods for you, all afraid to tell me you had disappeared. Save Frida, who came to me all a-tremble and said she feared some trickery. Your uncle was near as furious as I when we guessed the truth of it, and would have come with me to search for you. But he was forced to agree that this was for me to do and someone must stay behind to look to Erinwald. It was not difficult to know that de Brec must surely take you to Normandy, and I know the hills and this part of England far better than that Norman fool.' He almost spat the word. 'We came by another road, little known, to save time, but when the snow came I began to think I should lose all hope of finding you.'

He stopped and looked at her. 'And there's my tale. There is more I would tell you, of William and his court and of Saxons I met there, but let it wait. Are you now content? For you seem much recovered and I have a great desire to——'

A sudden glint of amusement gleamed in her eyes, and she held herself from him and said: 'Will we be able to return to Erinwald tomorrow? They must all be so worried.'

He looked at her in exasperation, torn between a desperate need for her, and a desire to be kind to her after all she had been through since he had snatched her so heedlessly from Erinwald that night.

Controlling himself with great difficulty, he answered: 'I do not know. The snow may keep us here for several days. Erinwald is safe in your uncle's keeping and when Olwyn returns with de Brec, he will be safely kept here until we can take him back for your uncle to deal with. That much I promised him,' he added grimly, 'though I'd as soon give him Saxon justice!'

He put a hand to her hair and entwined his fingers in it. 'But do not be in such haste, little one, for I have sworn to bring Ethelred and Vogar and Harald Erikson and others down from the hills to an allegiance with William, and must be about it soon.'

' 'Tis merely,' she returned solemnly, 'that I do not wish to be made truly your wife until we are at Erinwald; until we are home.'

He looked blankly at her, unable to believe what he had heard and obviously much displeased. 'Do you jest?'

'Nay,' she said, wide-eyed with innocence, 'but it would not be right.'

He struck a fist on the arm of the chair and stood up abruptly, walking away from her. 'Nay, wench! You ask too much! Do you think I am——?' He turned round to face her, his blue eyes full of fire, but she could control her features no longer, and at the sight of his contorted face she dissolved into laughter.

He crossed the room to her in swift strides, gripped her arms and pulled her roughly to her feet. 'You little vixen! I must needs teach you better, I think, than to tease your lord so!' He held her close against him and she felt a shudder go through him. With his mouth on her hair he said quietly, 'You should have pity on me, little one, for I am not made of iron, and 'tis many nights that I have slept in cold and empty beds thinking of you.'

He bent his head to kiss her neck gently, and

she caught her breath at the rush of sensations that coursed through her veins at his touch. How could she have teased him? How could she have held herself away from him, even for a second? She had thought him dead and lost to her, but here he was, alive and well and needing her in a way she barely understood, but which seemed to her at that moment more important than anything else. She put her arms up around his neck and clung to him as though she would never again release him.

He groaned softly as his mouth burned on hers in his hunger, and his hands sought the softness of her trembling body, caressing every curve with growing impatience. And his touch sent tingling shivers of pleasure through her until she thought she could bear it no longer.

Suddenly he tensed and pulled away from her with obvious difficulty. 'I do not want to tear this borrowed gown, wench,' he said hoarsely, 'but if you do not soon remove it, I fear it will end in shreds.'

She laughed softly, and very soon she had slipped out of the offending garment and stood naked before him, a little afraid of his great passion and her own trembling eagerness. But her slender body ached for him as she had not known it could, and she went more than willingly into his arms.

He picked her up and carried her to the bed, and stood for a moment letting his appreciative gaze take in every detail of her. ' 'Tis more than

time this marriage was consummated, witch,'
he said softly. 'What say you?'

Adela, her ordeals of the past day and night
quite forgotten, held out her arms invitingly to
him, and murmured, 'Yea, my lord.' But, being
Adela, she could not resist a little mischievous
smile, for she had suddenly lost her fear and
nervousness and was not at all apprehensive of
what was to come, and she added: 'But you
have had a long and tiring journey, my lord;
perhaps you are too weary and have not the
strength for it——?'

Anything else she might have said was lost in
a startled shriek, a gurgle of laughter and a
tangle of limbs, as she was left in very little
doubt on that score.

Masquerade
Historical Romances

Intrigue excitement romance

Don't miss
November's
other enthralling Historical Romance title

UNWILLING BETROTHAL
by Christine James

Annabelle Sarne is doubly an heiress — she will
inherit both her English grandmother's estates and
those of her French uncle, the Comte de Camoret.
But this, in pre-Revolutionary France, only doubles
her danger, and when the Comte is implicated in a
Royalist plot, Annabelle and her mother are forced
to flee to England. Their escape is aided by André, a
sinister French captain, who vanishes mysteriously.

Annabelle becomes fascinated by her unknown
rescuer, and dissatisfied with her betrothal to
Gaspard, Marquis d'Hubert — whom she thought she
loved. How can her heart change so quickly? And
who is the arrogant Englishman, apparently
connected with André, who threatens to deprive her
of Sarne Manor almost as soon as she arrives there?

You can obtain this title today from your local paperback
retailer

Masquerade
Historical Romances

Intrigue
excitement
romance

A PERFECT MATCH
by Julia Murray

Louisa married Simon, Lord Winslow, very reluctantly
indeed, and she knew that he had only offered for
her to preserve the proprieties. So why should he
interfere with her innocent attempts to help his
unhappy brother-in-law, Henry Landry?

FRENCHMAN'S HARVEST
by Emma Gayle

Helen Caister agreed to visit her mother's old home
— a château in the Médoc region of France — only
because she had fallen in love with her cousin, Marc
d'Auray, and could not refuse his invitation. But
Marc cared only for his inheritance and his precious
vines . . .

Look out for these titles in your local paperback shop from
12th December 1980

Doctor Nurse Romances

and November's
stories of romantic relationships behind the scenes
of modern medical life are:

DOCTORS IN CONFLICT
by Sonia Deane

It was love at first sight when Adam and Jessica met
in Amsterdam, and when he asked her to join his
practice in England it seemed like an invitation to
Paradise. But this Paradise, too, contained a serpent...

NURSE AT BARBAZON
(Summer at Barbazon)
by Kathryn Blair

Susan Day was asked to spend three months at a
Castelo in Portugal, as nurse-companion to a widowed
noblewoman. She was looking forward to her visit —
then she encountered the Castelo's imperious owner,
the Visconde Eduardo de Corte Ribeiro!

Order your copies today from your local paperback retailer

Masquerade
Historical Romances

Intrigue
excitement
romance

TARRISBROKE HALL
by Jasmine Cresswell

Utter ruin confronted the Earl of Tarrisbroke. Faced
with discharging his father's mountainous gambling
debts, what could he do but marry for money? But
the wife he chose, the wealthy young widow Marianne
Johnson, was not at all the vulgar title-hunting woman
he expected!

ZULU SUNSET
by Christina Laffeaty

Cassandra Hudson wanted to be a missionary's wife —
more particularly, her cousin Martin's wife. So she
travelled to Zululand to visit him, confident that her
new fortune would smooth her way. Unfortunately
she found herself in the midst of an impending war
between whites and Zulus, and the only man who
could help her reach Martin was the odious, arrogant
Saul Parnell . . .

**These titles are still available through your local paperback
retailer**